AMERICAN 587 HEAVY

A NOVEL OF TERRORISM AND BETRAYAL

HOWARD J. SCHWACH

To Susi, who was my inspiration until she passed, to Rob and Amy, who have taken care of me since and to my grandchildren, Ryan, Corey and Lauren, who have always been there when I needed them.

AUTHOR'S NOTE

"American 587 Heavy" is work of fiction. While the genesis of the idea for this novel was a real-life event, the crash of American Airlines Flight 587 into the streets of the middle-class Belle Harbor (New York City) community on November 12, 2001, just two months and a day after the fall of the two World Trade Center buildings, the characters in this novel, and especially the events that follow the crash are fictional and exist only in the author's mind.

None of the characters are real. While some Rockaway residents may believe that they see themselves or other local residents in the book, most are amalgams of many people who live in Rockaway, while others embody the attributes and character of people both in and outside of New York City that the author has met in his 76 years on this globe. Still others are made up of whole cloth.

Having said that, many of the words spoken by those characters, particularly those in the cockpit of American 587 Heavy prior to the crash, as well as those of air traffic control and first responders, are taken directly from the records and transcripts of such agencies as the Federal Aviation Administration (FAA), National Transportation Safety Board (NTSB), New York Police Department (NYPD) and the Fire Department of New York (FDNY). Those words, spoken first by those actually involved in the AA 587 incident, are used not to prove any complicity in the act, but to add authenticity to the book. And, while The Beachcomber newspaper sounds much like The Wave, the local newspaper edited by the author for more than a decade, they are not identical and changes have been made for literary reasons.

The official cause of the crash, as decided by the NTSB in

October of 2004, was the "unnecessary and aggressive use of the aircraft's rudder" by the first officer, who was flying the departure from John F. Kennedy Airport that day. As contributing factors, the NTSB listed both American Airline's pilot training program and the rudder system developed by Airbus Industries. Those reports had never found widespread traction in the Rockaway community, particularly on the part of the dozens of eyewitnesses, many of them trained observers such as firefighters and police officers. Their reports or fire and explosion while the plane was still in the air, disdained by the NTSB as "unreliable," still fuel more sinister theories about why American Airlines Flight 587 crashed that day, killing all 260 people on the plane and five on the ground while destroying several homes. Those theories still abound both in the Rockaway community and the wider community that sees conspiracy at every turn.

Those theories have been fueled more recently by media reports of terrorist activity, of an Muslim Jihadist in the hands of Canadian security services who says that AA 587 was brought down by the second "shoe bomber," naming for the act a man who has been missing since before November 12, 2001 and is still wanted by the FBI today.

I have obviously taken liberties and literary license in presenting the events both leading up to the crash and subsequent to the crash in this fictional novelization of a real-life event. There will be some in the community who may well be angered by the publication of this book, a fictional work about an event that changed their lives forever, even more than fifteen years after the event. For those who are angered, I apologize in advance for any pain that this book may have caused them. It is meant, however, to be a paean to the memory of all who died that day, to all of those both on and off-duty, who responded to assist the people of Belle Harbor.

Belle Harbor, New York City
August, 2018

I

"It is a good day to die, a good day to enter Paradise," Shafiq Sa Hamad thought.

It was a pleasant day for November, especially for New York City, where the weeks prior to Thanksgiving often resemble winter rather than fall, and especially so in a large open area right on Jamaica Bay, where the wind often blows off the water with a sting that can make it seem 10 or even 20 degrees colder early in the winter.

This morning, the sun was warming and the wind was not at all uncomfortable, not what he was told to expect when he was briefed by Omar in the safe house in Kabul just two months ago.

Just being on the water, feeling the gentle roll of the boat, was slightly unsettling, however, a little disorienting, making him slightly dizzy. He didn't like the feeling, wanted to get this whole episode over with. Wanted it to end. Today! One way or the other. Death or dishonor.

He chided himself. Was the uneasy feeling because of the boat's motion, a situation he had never experienced, or was it what he was about to do?

He laughed quietly to himself.

"Mass murder, even for a cause such as his, would make anybody unsettled," he thought.

Hopefully, his mission would end with success and he would never have to feel the rocking of any accursed boat again.

1

It's not that he was a coward. He had proven his bravery numerous times against the enemies of Islam, both on battlefields and in operations against the Great Satan around the world. None of his previous operations had been like this one. Not as large, not as important.

"This is the one I have trained for," he reassured himself. "I can do this and then return home to fight again.

He silently recited a passage from the Quorn and then, almost as an inspiration, he remembered a long-forgotten portion of an Arab war song - The Death Feud -- that that he had learned in the camps and that always gave him strength. He believed was just like that Arab Bedouin in the war song, riding his camel across the desert, with only his blooded sword as a companion, riding to do battle with the infidels who covets his domain.

Except he wasn't on a camel and he wasn't on the desert. He was in a place called Brooklyn and he was on a small boat. He recited the poem to himself, struggling to remember all the words that he had been taught long ago.

"Terrible he rode alone
With only his Yemen sword for aid;
Ornament, it had none
But the notches on the blade."

The boat began to rock more violently as a larger boat passed by about one hundred yards offshore, bringing him back from his reverie to the reality of where he was, what he was about to do.

He hated boats and thought that everything about large bodies of water sucked. He thought that it was ironic that this boat, owned by a devout Muslim, who lived nearby the marina in the Howard Beach community in Queens, was called "Last Call," which he was told was some sort of reference to drinking alcohol in a bar, something that was forbidden to true Muslims.

Perhaps he would settle a debt with the boat's owner for his affront before going home. If he survived today's action. If he covered himself in glory.

The slightly-built Jihadist liked to use words like "sucked" and "bogus," words that he thought of as "American, as "cool."

He used American slang whenever he could, even though he hated Americans and their corrupt ways, because using them lessened the chance that he would be seen as an outsider, less chance that he would be stopped and questioned by the dreaded police. That was the last thing Shafiq needed, at least for several more hours. Then, one way or another, it would all be over. Despite the fact that it was not at all cold, he pulled his down jacket closer to his chest, pulled the zipper up towards his throat, and shuddered involuntarily.

The only water Tafiq found pleasing was the kind you could get from a well or a bottle, the kind you could drink. Perhaps, that came from growing up in a series of Palestinian refugee camps run by the United Nations, growing up bristling under Israeli control, without ever having enough clean water to drink or food to eat, seeing his mother and father degraded by the Jews, by his brother Arabs, feeling the oppressor's boot. Listening to the Imams in the local Madrassa, who preached not love and tolerance, but Jihad, death and destruction. Today, he assured himself, he would fulfill his destiny.

He looked around at his surroundings, at the large bridge to his south, at the expanse of bay to his west and the small airport control tower across a four-lane road, Flatbush Avenue, a road which separated the marina from a large unused airport that was once used by the military but that was now part of a national park. So unlike home, he thought. So unlike anywhere he had ever been before.

Despite his hatred of America, here he was, early in the morning, with a light fog hanging over Jamaica Bay and the Barren Island Marina, getting ready to take a short ride on a small, 23-foot boat that might well be the last ride he ever took, a means of transportation that might bring him to glory or that might bring him to Allah and to paradise, to the promise that being a martyr for his people and his God would bring.

It made no difference to Tafiq. He had cleansed himself, made his peace and was as prepared for the rewards of martyrdom as he was for the rewards of the flesh.

Yet, he had questions that were unresolved even within himself.

"What am I doing here, so far from home," he asked aloud, more to himself than to his partner, Sayed el-wed, who was standing only a few feet away, still on the marina dock, taking their weapons from the rear cargo space of their rented Chevrolet Tahoe SUV. "Do I really want to kill all those people?"

Almost as an answer, Sayed, who was taking their equipment bags from the car, spoke quietly as always, but loudly enough for him to hear.

"Come and help me here," he said. "We have to get these weapons into the boat and out of sight before somebody becomes suspicious and asks to look at our fishing rods or at the permits we probably need to fish in the bay. We don't have a lot of time."

Tafiq awkwardly climbed out of the boat, balancing on the gunwale and jumping to the wooden dock. He walked the short distance to the rear of the car, wishing once more that he had Sayed's faith, wished that he didn't have his doubts. He looked inside the SUV's large cargo area, spotting the assault rifle and the two long, cylindrical green tubes, each about six feet in length, which lay on the cargo deck. Even knowing in advance that they were there, their appearance caused his heart to skip a beat and he wondered again if he was up to actually doing what he had trained to do.

Tafiq grabbed the AK-47 assault rifle and one of the tubes, turned, and began to walk to the boat. Sayed grabbed the other tube, loudly slammed the trunk and followed Tafiq from the parking lot down the short wooded pier to the boat.

The local television news they had watched in the Brooklyn safe house the night before had reported that it would be a clear and relatively warm day. The beautiful, young woman who was doing the weather report also said that it was a holiday in America, something called "Veteran's Day," and that many schools, banks and post offices would be closed, although most stores would be open, hold-ing large sales.

He wondered why a holiday honoring veterans would be best known for special sales in large stores. Just one more thing about Americans that he did not understand. One among many.

While his partner worried that a holiday for veterans might bring out lots of police and soldiers and extra surveillance, Tafiq doubted that it would cause any problems for them in carrying out their mission. At least, the weather would be no problem. The vis-ibility would be perfect and they would have no problem focusing on their prey.

Allah was with them, as always. Perhaps that was a sign to in-sure that his faith was strong, Tafiq thought.

He was assured by his handlers that the boat was typical of those used on the bay and would draw no interest unless they did something out of the ordinary to attract somebody's attention to them.

His handlers – his money men who had funded his trip to New York, his apartment, his weapons, his food and everything else – including some prostitutes – were important, involved with the September 11 action as well.

He had personally met only one of his shadowy handlers. His name was Omar al-Bayoumi, and he was reputedly with Saudi intel-ligence, something that Tafiq thought from experience was prob-ably true. Certainly, his pockets were deep and his contacts, even in New York City, were many.

Tafiq had heard from others that Omar had handled Khalid al-Mihdar and Nawfi al-Talzmi, two of the 9/11 hijackers when they were in San Diego, California, awaiting their chance to hijack an air-liner and carry out their mission. Now Omar was living on Atlantic Avenue in Brooklyn, helping with this mission, less important than 9/11 perhaps, but important in its own way in striking a blow against the Great Satan.

Tafiq had met Omar only once. He and his partner were ordered to go to a Jewish restaurant on Second Avenue in Manhattan at a specified time and day. Omar showed up "accidently" while they were waiting to be served. While they ate halal food, he passed along a change in orders and information on where the boat and the weapons could be found, who his local contacts – his compatriots who would feed them, find them an apartment, supply transportation and the like -- would be. The meeting was anything but accidental, but his choice of restaurants and Omar's accidental appearance reassured Tafiq that everything was well-planned.

If Omar and Allah were truly with them, he believed, the blow they were preparing to strike this morning might well be the second step on his people's road back to Palestine and an end to accursed Israel and all the Jew who lived there. The first, of course, and the greatest was an event that had happened only two months ago, the attack on the World Trade Center, a blow that led to the collapse of both great buildings and had shook the confidence of the Great Satan. Tafiq's blow would be the second, albeit not as great in terms of the loss of life and property suffered by Satan in Manhattan, which they could see across the bay.

Tafiq and then Sayed dropped their weapons into the boat, taking care not to unduly jar the cylindrical tubes. They were warned during training in Afghanistan that the tubes were not dangerous until armed, but that you could never be too sure around explosives, especially exotic rocket launchers that had probably originally come from America itself in its support of bin-Laden and the others when they were fighting with the American CIA against the Russian invaders in Afghanistan many years ago. They were old and unstable, they were told, and it was best not to handle them too roughly until it was actually time to use them.

Both men went back to the car, and each took a fishing rod from the back seat. Neither had ever used a fishing rod, but their training, they hoped, had given them enough information and expertise to fool any other fishermen out on the bay that day or any police officer who made a cursory inspection of the boat or who saw them once they were in position on Jamaica Bay.

By 8:15 a.m., they were ready to push off from the Barren

Island Marina. Tafiq took one more look around, more to screw up his courage than to insure that they were not being observed. A few boats were leaving the marina at the same time, some turning east into the bay, others moving west towards the point of land that would lead them to the Atlantic Ocean.

Across Flatbush Avenue, Floyd Bennett Field was quiet, so quiet that they could not see a single person through the gate, nor were there any sounds coming from the field, expect for an occasional police helicopter that lifted off from the bay side of the field and then quickly went elsewhere. It was clear that nobody had taken note of them and their small boat among all the others. Many people kept their fishing boats at the marina and the weather was still warm enough for many of those fishermen to be out on the bay on a nice holiday morning. They would attract no attention if they followed their instructions to the letter.

As they were taught, Sayed started the boat's engine and they motored south, breaking out fishing rods so that it would look as if they were simply two men out for a day's holiday fishing before the winter weather settled in. In fact, there were a few other boats on the water. They had worried that the weather would be bad and they would be the only boat on the bay, making them an easy target for somebody who wanted to check to see what they were doing.

He took a last look at the rental car, parked nearby the dock, which he would never see again, wondering how long it would take the rental car company to find it.

They motored south for a few minutes and then turned eastward past the gated community of Breezy Point, a grouping of small homes and bungalows, they were told, where many police and firefighters lived. While they worried that people might be watching them from the beach that separated the homes from the bay, there was nobody on the beach as they motored eastward, leaving the large, white beach behind and passing under the Gil Hodges-Marine Parkway Bridge into Jamaica Bay itself.

When Tafiq had studied the map he had been given in Brooklyn, he wondered aloud who Gil Hodges was. His handlers shrugged. They did not know, and it really wasn't important. Probably some decadent politician who was responsible for building the bridge, Tafiq thought, or some war hero. For some reason, he wished that he had found out. Now, it would probably be too late.

To the south as they slowly motored eastward under the high bridge was a now-abandoned Coast Guard station and then the Rockaway peninsula, a finger of land that was surrounded by water – Jamaica Bay to the north and the Atlantic Ocean to the south. At this point, Floyd Bennett Field was to the left, with row upon row of single-family homes on the Rockaway peninsula to the right. They had been told not to worry about a quick response from the field. The police helicopters that were housed just across the bay seldom came south unless they were called, and only an old and unarmed U.S. Parks Police boat was now stationed at the former Coast Guard Station. Due to budget cuts, the coast guard boats and helicopters had been moved to New Jersey and to the eastern end of Long Island. There would be no military presence nearby the bay that day.

Their briefer had told them to find a place in the center of the bay, north of a restaurant called "The Rockaway Sunset Diner," which they would be able to clearly see from the bay, and south of a large marsh area called "Grassy Bay" on their maps.

Planes departing John F. Kennedy Airport's Runway 31 Left regularly flew right over that spot, depending on the wind and the time of day. They had been told, however, that early in the morning in November, the winds would favor large jets using the runway designated on their maps as 31 Left and that they could expect lots of targets, large commercial airliners flying low and slow on their departure runs, still struggling for altitude.

After a few minutes, Tafiq saw in the distance to his left the control tower for John F. Kennedy Airport and then, a minute later, on his right, the Sunset Diner on the Rockaway bay front, right where it was supposed to be. It heartened him that the planning for the mission had been extensive, leaving them little to do but carry out their orders.

Despite the light chill on the water, Tafiq felt sweat trickling down his chest under the sweatshirt and jacket he had recently purchased in Brooklyn.

Both he and his partner, as they had been told to do, had chosen sweatshirts bearing the logos of New York City's professional baseball teams, Tafiq, the "Yankees," and Sayed, a team called. "The Mets." They had expected that it would be much colder, especially on the water and the sweat shirts had the dual advantage of being local camouflage. They had seen many local men and children, even women, wearing similar shirts in the two weeks they spent in Brooklyn. They were told that the baseball season had just ended and that nobody would look twice at somebody wearing local team shirts.

Both men sat in the boat as it rocked slowly back and forth and looked towards the airport.

Tafiq wondered if they would need binoculars to see the planes, but were assured that the planes would be large enough and low enough to see clearly.

As if to confirm that, a large jet plane lifted off from the airport, and could clearly be seen making a left turn over the bay, heading right for them. When the plane, an Airbus A320, bearing the logo of JetBlue Airlines passed over them, it was at about 10,000 feet, well within the range of their weapon.

They turned their heads slowly and followed the plane with their eyes as it disappeared over the Rockaway peninsula and then quickly over the Atlantic Ocean.

The peninsula was only five short blocks wide in that area.

They had some time to spare. Their orders were to bring down a large airliner. It didn't matter to them or to the planners back in Afghanistan what plane they chose, as long as it was an American-flag passenger plane large enough to carry a few hundred people. That was all they needed. That they were going to do it on a day designated by the devils as "Veterans Day," a day to honor those who fought for the great Satan, was an added incentive.

Tafiq looked around. He looked towards the Rockaway shore.

He could see that a wide commercial street that ran from the diner north towards the beachfront. Many cars passed by on the street that ran from east to west, between the diner and the bay wall. Out of curiosity and a lack of anything else to do, he took out his map and found the street. It was called Beach Channel Drive, not Bay Channel Drive, as he would have expected. It was another American mystery that would never be answered.

At that time on a November morning, there would not be too many people in the area especially on a holiday morning, other than those having breakfast in the diner, they were told.

Being so close to the diner was a risk that they had to take. They needed to be close to the plane and the spot offshore of that diner was the perfect spot for a direct head-on kill.

It was nearly 9:15. Time to get ready. Tafiq opened one of the green cylinders and fingered the weapon inside. He pulled it free from the tube, grabbing the trigger mechanism as he had been taught. The smooth feel of the metal made him tingle with anticipation. Soon, he would fire the weapon and hundreds would die.

II

B ob Molshin walked around the large aircraft, touching the aluminum skin of the plane as if he were touching a woman, feeling for impurities, for dents and dings, for any anomaly or movement that would cause him problems while he was in the air.

He studied the landing gear and particularly the tires for wear or spots where the rubber was completely gone. He was a happy camper today, after a couple of days on the beach that left much to be desired, with too much to drink, too much to eat and too few women. He was glad that he was going back into the air.

To Molshin, his pre-flight routine was almost as exciting as fore-play with a woman, almost a sexual act. The act of pre-flighting an aircraft, he thought to his great chagrin, was an act that he had probably preformed much more often in his long flying career than he had actual sexual encounters. There was no denying the fact. The walk-around of an aircraft before flight always gave him a natural high. Behind the stick of a fast-mover was his environment, the reason he was born.

Like many ex-military pilots, Molshin was not a large man at five foot, nine inches, but his military bearing and his close-cropped dark hair and trimmed mustache, added to his slim build and the squared-away cut of his uniform, always marked him as an ex-military pilot. He just had that "look" that many of the ex-military pilots that had transitioned to civilian life after long careers of flying off aircraft carriers or into hot landing zones seem to have even years after their last encounters with military duty.

Of course, the leather flight jacket adorned with the squadron and ship's patches detailing his Navy years might have been another clue to any of the dozens of men and women working around the plane, getting it ready to take to the air.

Molshin had been walking circles around fast-movers, checking for problems before take-off, for a long time. It had been years, perhaps far too many years, since he strapped on his first Tomcat on the USS Enterprise back on that long-ago 1987 Mediterranean cruise. Where had those 14 years gone?

"God, I'm getting old fast in a young man's game," he thought, not for the first time, rubbing the struts to make sure they were sufficiently greased. He tried to make sure that nothing untoward escaped his glance, even though highly-trained mechanics had recently done the exact checks.

It had been like that from the beginning, he thought, first at flight training in Pensacola and then at a series of squadrons with a variety of Naval aircraft.

To the compact, well-muscled pilot, it seemed like only yesterday that he was launching from the Enterprise's massive flight deck on interdiction missions in the no-fly zone over Iraq. Now, he flew happy, excited civilians home to the Dominican Republic for the holidays.

Something of a let-down, but it was a job and it was flying, albeit not a very exciting variety of flying.

The feeling of elation, of a heightened awareness that he would soon take the bird in front of him into the air, however, dimmed his skepticism and made him slightly euphoric.

He supposed that he would always have those feelings about flight, no matter how many birds he flew, no matter that this one was not a state-of-the-art U.S. Navy fast mover, but an American Airlines passenger plane, built by a French company that cared more for passenger comfort and profit than for the pilot's enjoyment.

He would soon strap himself into the left-hand seat of an Airbus

A300-600 and take 260 men, women and children to their homes and vacation hotels in the warmth of the DR.

The good-looking captain continued his walk-around, checking the control surfaces of the aircraft. He quickly glanced at the tail number high above him – N14053. He looked at the flight manifest on the clipboard he carried under his right elbow to make sure this was his bird.

"Of all the things that could go wrong with a flight, they've never given me the wrong bird," he thought, with a grin.

As usual, the exterior of the A300 was crawling with people. There were company techs making last minute checks and last minute fixes, fuel handlers gassing the airplane with JP-5 fuel for the long flight south, food handlers bringing lunches and drinks for the 250 passengers and crew, baggage handlers loading the first of the long trains of baggage carts brought from the American Airlines Terminal at John F. Kennedy Airport, much of it already stacked in the large hold below the passenger area of the plane.

Molshin glanced around, watching the activity around him, once again amazed by the number of people it took to get a plane into the air. He was just about finished with his inspection of the plane, satisfied that it was ready for flight.

"Are we ready to go," a voice behind him asked. "Everything check out OK?

"Hey, Carl, you're guess is as good as mine," he told his first officer, Carl Shades. He and the diminutive Shades had shared a number of long, over-water flights to and from the island and he felt comfortable joking with him about the readiness of the plane. "Everything taken care of on your end?"

Shades glanced at the plane. While not ex-military, he was a no-nonsense pilot in his own right, trained as a teenager by his dad, an Eastern Airlines pilot. A good stick and a good companion on the long overwater flight. "The flight plan is filed. We're nominal at the gate. We take the bridge climb and then circle to port. Our first waypoint is WAVEY. The weather looks nominal, fuel state is nominal, I checked the NOTAMS and there is just one thing that we have to be concerned about," Shades said, clearly happy that the necessary paperwork details were completed and they would soon get into the air.

NOTAMS were "Notices to Airmen," issued by the FAA, detailing changes in procedure or unusual situations that the pilots should be aware of. One of the last things that pilots did before departing an airport, even a familiar one, was to check the latest NOTAMS.

"The new departure rules require that we climb pretty quickly, about 500 feet per nautical mile," Shades added. "I guess the natives in Rockaway have been complaining to the FAA about us flying too low over their homes again, making too much noise and waking them up, bothering them on the beach. Should be no problem though, in this weather and at our weight. We depart on 31 left, behind a JAL heavy. We're ready to go if the aircraft is."

Molshin shook his head in the affirmative to indicate that he understood as much as to agree that the unusually steep climb would be no problem on this flight. He was slightly unhappy, however, that the NOTAM required them to take the A300 a little steeper than he liked. Like most pilots, he did not like last minute changes, especially when they worked against the safety of the aircraft – and of the passengers. He knew, however, that the FAA had to keep the natives who lived nearby the airport happy, and low flights over expensive homes made for a very unhappy group of residents.

"How are you feeling," he asked Shades, concerned slightly that his first officer had the beginnings of a bad cold two days before when they had flown into New York. States said he was going to take some meds while they were laying over in the Big City.

Molshin was not making idle small talk, but checking on the fitness of his first officer to fly the departure that day.

"Fine," Shades answered tersely. "No problem."

"Did ATC tell you if we have any military-type fast-movers flying high cover for us today," the captain asked, changing the subject. Navy F-14 Tomcats and Air Force F-15 Strike Eagles had been constantly flying racetrack patterns over both New York City and Washington, D.C. for the past two months, ever since the terrorist attacks that brought down the World Trade Center and damaged the Pentagon in Washington, D.C.

While the ex-Navy pilot enjoyed watching military jets in flight, it also made him angry that military pilots had to waste their time flying around over New York City when they could be doing useful work in Afghanistan, seeking out those who ordered the September attacks on America.

"There should be some Toms' from the Teddy Roosevelt to our south," Shades answered. "They'll stay clear of us unless we squawk a problem, and then they'll be on us quick enough."

Molshin secretly hoped that some F-14 Tomcats, the Navy's front-line fighter-interceptor would wander over to his flight, American Flight 587, to take a look. He had flown Tomcats, a high-performance jet fighter for the VF-14 "Tophatter's" and those supersonic fighter aircraft were his first love. Certainly, more so than the Airbus, which he considered a bitch of an aircraft to fly, a plane with unexplained rudder control problems.

He had even given some thought to bidding with the union to move back to the 747's, but that would have meant a cut in pay or perhaps a move to another city. He was not ready for either of those eventualities, so he continued to fly the A300, even if he was not happy about it.

As if Shades was reading his mind, he asked, "I hear through the grapevine that you are thinking of dropping this route. Is that true, or just the usual bum skinny," using the military slang for a rumor. "It's just a thought that I had," the captain replied. "I don't know exactly why, but I'm just not real sure of this aircraft anymore. There was that PIA A300 that went down in late '92 that killed 167. About 250 were killed when that A300 went down in Indonesia in '97. There was that fishtailing incident in Florida where a stew broke her back. There have been too many accidents where somebody was hurt or where the plane was brought down at an alternative airport somewhere because of control problems."

The two men climbed the gangway that had been placed near the front of the aircraft and went directly to the cabin to preflight the plane. The first of the passengers would be boarding in a few minutes, and the company was always concerned with "on-time" departures. The plane was due to be wheels up at 9:29 Eastern Standard Time, and Molshin was concerned that he could pull off an on-time departure.

Those who worked with him knew him as a by-the-book aircraft commander. He was. It was probably a carryover from his Navy days, when carrier operations, especially those carried out at night, could kill quickly if a pilot did not understand all the rules and did not fly his aircraft strictly by the book.

Both Molshin and Shades slipped into their seats – Molshin on the left and Shades on the right – and strapped in. They began to move through the written preflight checklist. Both had been through it so often that it had become boring and rote, and they could probably do the checklist from memory, but they ran through the checklist and every time as if it were the first time.

The cockpit door was open and the two men could hear the passengers coming aboard, putting their carry-on luggage away and getting settled. The flight attendants, aware of Molshin's proclivity for concentration, stayed away from the cockpit while the preflight was being completed.

Shades was going to fly the departure that day. Molshin considered it one of his major roles as a command pilot that he mentor younger, less experienced pilots. He often allowed his first officers, all of whom were qualified pilots in their own right, albeit with less experience than him, to take the plane out of an airport. Many other captains did not.

Shades was particularly experienced for a young first officer. He would soon be promoted to captain, probably with the next opening. He was a good stick and thoroughly checked out on the A-300 as well as a few other aircraft in the American Airline stable.

Shades had been monitoring ground control as he worked the complicated checklist. He listened as Kennedy Ground called the JAL plane lined up in front of them for takeoff. Soon, it would be their turn.

"Kennedy ground, Japan Air forty-seven heavy ready for taxi, we have echo," he heard as the next aircraft in the pattern, a Japan Airlines 747, prepared for takeoff.

"Japan air forty seven heavy, Kennedy ground. Runway 31 Left for departure. Taxi left on Bravo and, uh, hold short of, uh, kilo kilo," Kennedy ground control responded.

"Left on bravo, hold short of kilo kilo, three one left Japan Air forty seven," the cockpit of the JAL plane acknowledged.

"Japan four seven heavy, monitor the tower one, one, niner, niner point one. So long."

"One, one, niner niner point one, rolling. So long, sir."

Both Molshin and Shades tightened their seatbelts and readied themselves for takeoff.

"American 587 heavy, follow the Japan Air heavy Boeing 747 ahead. Monitor the tower one, one, niner niner point one," ground control ordered.

Shades quickly responded.

"Follow Japan air over to tower eleven nineteen one. American 587."

"American 587 heavy, Kennedy Tower. Caution, wake turbulence runway 31 left. Taxi into position and hold."

"Position and hold, thirty-one left, American 587 heavy."

"American 587 Heavy, wind three zero zero at niner. Runway three one left cleared for takeoff," the local controller high in the tower told the aircraft's pilots. It was exactly 9:29, Molshin noted. Although he was a minute or two from wheels up, he felt somehow comforted by the thought that he was departing nearly on time.

"Cleared for takeoff, American, ah, 587 heavy," Shades responded, confirming the orders and telling local control that they were ready to roll.

"American 587 Heavy, plane is rolling," Shades added as he pushed the throttles to the first stop. The plane rolled quickly down the runway, reaching takeoff velocity, what pilots call "V-1." Shades pulled back on the stick.

The plane lifted off and Molshin pulled up the wheels. Their departure was officially two minutes late.

Within seconds, American Airlines Flight 587 was at 800 feet over Jamaica Bay, flying at 159 knots. Molshin and Shades, along with the passengers and crew aboard the flight, had only 80 seconds to live.

"American 587 Heavy, turn left. Fly the bridge climb. Contact New York Departure, Good Morning," the local controller said.

"American 587 Heavy, thank you and so long," Molshin, who was now handling the radios while Shades was flying the departure, answered.

The plane was now at 1,200 feet and flying at 161 knots.

Molshin contacted departure control.

"Uh, New York, American 587 Heavy, 1300 feet. Climbing to five thousand.

Departure control, what pilots call TRACON, situated in Freeport, Long Island, about 16 miles east of the airport, replied.

"American 587 Heavy, New York departure radar contact. Climb and maintain one three thousand."

"One three, that's for American 587 Heavy," Molshin responded into his microphone, assuring the FAA that he had received their instructions and confirming that they had him on radar.

The aircraft was now 33 seconds into its flight, at 2,700 feet and traveling at 170 knots. It was 70 seconds from disaster.

The two pilots felt a slight shudder in the aircraft.

"What the hell was that," Shades asked, attempting to trim the plane.

"Must be some turbulence from JAL 47, the heavy that took off just before we did," Molshin responded, although he was not sure that the shudder was the result of wave vortex left behind by the Japan Airlines plane.

Seconds later TRACON contacted the plane again.

"American 587, turn left, proceed direct WAVEY," the controller ordered.

Shades responded to the movement of the plane, which was

now turning directly south over Jamaica Bay towards the Rockaway peninsula, at the same time feeling another shudder in the aircraft.

"Uh, uh, turn direct WAVEY, American 587 Heavy," Molshin responded, not sure whether he should tell the controller of the problems with the aircraft.

Shades inputted the WAVEY designation into the flight computer. WAVEY was a computer-generated code word for a designated departure point, called a waypoint by pilots, over the ocean about thirty miles southeast of the Rockaway peninsula. Planes departing JFK and then heading south to Latin or South America used WAVEY regularly as a designated departure point.

"Take her off the Breezy Track and fly directly over Rockaway to WAVEY," Molshin said, following TRACON's direction.

The change from the bridge climb route that would have taken the plane over Jamaica Bay, west over the Marine Parkway Bridge at the tip of the Rockaway peninsula and away from the homes of Rockaway was not unusual.

The Bridge Climb took the departing planes away from the row upon row of one and two-family homes that made up the Belle Harbor and the more expensive Neponsit communities on the peninsula. The residents who lived in those middle-class and upper middle-class communities loved the bridge climb or "Breezy Track," which allowed departing aircraft from 31L to stay away from residential areas, but the both the pilots and the airlines disliked it because it added time and fuel costs to the flight.

At the same time that States turned the A-300 to fly directly over Jamaica Bay, Sayed was holding a fishing pole, with its line in the waters of that same bay. Anybody looking at the boat from the shore would believe them to be late season fishermen enjoying a day on the water – or so they hoped.

It was time to get ready.

Tafiq's heart was racing as he reached down and took one of the missile launchers, trying to keep it low enough so that it was out of sight, below the boat's gunwales. He fingered the sight to make sure it was aligned correctly and then the trigger.

They had told him that the Stinger Missile, an American-made weapon that was given widely to the freedom fighters in Afghanistan by the American CIA, was reliable up to several miles. He would not need that much range today. With clear skies, few waves rocking the boat and a plane lower than 30,000 feet above and coming straight at them, this would be an optimum shot. Much easier than the practice dry-fire shots with test missiles he had made in the camp. He felt a tingle in his arms as he lifted the deadly missile. His arms felt weak, but he managed to shoulder it with little difficulty.

"I'm really going to do this," he said to himself, as much a question as a statement.

As he removed the Stinger missile from its case, a loud roar startled Tafiq. He looked up and saw a smaller, needle-nosed aircraft barrel southward across the bay in a hurry, its nose tilted down like a praying mantis in the hunt.

The noise of the plane as it passed over him was overwhelming, but he had no time to watch the beautiful aircraft climb away. He had work to do.

He turned again to his task. He was told specifically not to bring down a supersonic Concorde. First of all, it would belong to either the French or the British, not to the Americans. Second of all, it contained many fewer passengers than a large American jetliner.

He easily lifted the 35-pound weapon, which was already loaded with a "fire and forget" supersonic missile. The high-speed missile, which was developed by the U.S. Army to shoot down helicopters and low-flying jet planes, had a passive infrared sensor that would lock into and follow the largest heat source available. An engine on a large jetliner made the perfect heat source. The missile's proximity fuse would explode not far from the engine, blowing shrapnel and explosive forces into the fuselage of the large aircraft.

Tafiq hefted the weapon on his shoulder and looked through

the sight at the end of the airport's runway, and then at his watch. It was 9:23.

"The next American plane is the one," he thought.

He saw a plane take off from the airport and turn in his direction. He had been trained to spot the tail of the plane to tell what nation it came from. This plane, he could see from the large, red "Rising Sun" on the tail was a JAL 747 – Japan Airlines. He let it pass.

They watched as the next plane took off, looking for its tail markings as it began its climb-out from the airport. This was it, it he thought. The large red and blue double "A's" on the tail told him that it was an American Airlines jetliner. How fitting it would be that he brought down a plane belonging to the national carrier of the county he wanted so much to destroy.

He waited a minute or two as the plane turned to the left, right towards him. When it was nearly overhead, he looked through the launcher's sight at the plane and pulled the trigger to the first stop. He heard a tone that told him that the missile had acquired the aircraft. He pulled the trigger to the second and final stop, and the missile leaped from the tube with a roar and a trail of smoke, almost knocking him off the rocking boat's fantail.

Tafiq looked in fascination as the missile headed for the American Airlines plane. He knew that the missile was going to knock down the aircraft. He threw the launcher into the bay, as he had been told to do. Sayed did the same with the second Stinger, followed by the AK-47. They no longer needed the missile launchers since the first one operated as promised and, if they were discovered now, a firefight was the last thing they wanted.

They turned the boat to the north, heading for the channel that would take them back to Howard Beach and a mooring behind Russo's On the Bay Catering Hall. It was a much shorter trip than going back to Brooklyn, and they would leave the boat there for its owners to retrieve. Then, as they had been told to do, they would make their way to the A-Train subway stop at Howard Beach and return to the safe house in Brooklyn.

The two men heard a clap of thunder in the clear sky as the

speeding missile with its proximity fuse exploded behind the plane's starboard wing, about half-way to the tail. They watched for a moment as the plane shuddered and skewed westward. The plane's tail ripped off and fell away, quickly spiraling into the waters of the bay.

"One last time in the Brooklyn safe house with Zeata," Tafiq thought, and then to the airport and home. He would miss Zeata. She somehow sensed that he would soon be a martyr, and that made their sexual activity all the better. She was tough, but tender, the operative who had rented the car for them, bought them food and provided him gratification. He would miss her greatly. There was nobody for him like that wherever he would wind up – except in paradise. He wished that he could have had more time with her or that she could go back to Afghanistan with him, but neither of those were possibilities. Perhaps he would come back to Brooklyn one day on another mission or when the Great Satan was over and the world was Muslim.

It would be great to get home, however, to stop looking over his shoulder 24 hours a day. He would be a true hero to his people for what he did today. "Much better than being a martyr," he thought to himself, as he shrugged and looked forward to the trip to Howard Beach. He would not be going to paradise this day.

Once the missile was in the air, neither Tafiq nor Sayed had any further interest in American Airlines Flight 587 traveling from New York City to the Dominican Republic and carrying 260 passengers and a full crew of five, an airliner that had only seconds to live.

———— ((●)) ————

The two pilots heard a louder noise near the starboard wing, and Flight 587 suddenly accelerated sideways. It went into a slight flat spin to the west.

"That's got to be wake vortex," Molshin said, not suspecting that a missile had exploded near the starboard wing, but toying with the idea of taking control back from Shades.

"Do you have control," he asked Shades.

"I've got it," his first officer responded, though the sweat on his brow indicated to Molshin that it might be otherwise.

"TRACON, we are experiencing wake vortex," Molshin said into his microphone.

"Try escape?" Shades asked Molshin, asking the more experienced pilot for help.

When pilots "try escape," because a plane is experiencing wind shear or wake vortex turbulence, the book requires them to go through a set of pre-determined maneuvers.

Those procedures call for disabling the autopilot and the auto-throttle, rotating the nose up by fifteen degrees and applying maximum power

"Maximum Power," Shades said, moving his hands to the throttles, while at the same time checking the autopilot and auto-throttle, both of which were off. He pulled on the wheel to rotate the nose fifteen degrees.

Rather than reducing the shudder, however, the lateral movements only increased.

The plane began to fishtail, giving the passengers their first hint that something was wrong with the aircraft.

"What are we in," Shades asked.

"Get out of it, get out of it," Molshin responded with some panic in his voice.

"Losing control," the air traffic controller at TRACON heard from the cockpit of flight 587, buried among other garbled transmissions. The plane and those on it had 15 seconds to live.

————))((————

Carol Luczak allowed her tense muscles to relax a little bit.

"OK, take it easy," she said to herself. "We're off the ground and everything is fine. No problems. Breathe easy and relax."

Early in her career as a buyer for Saks Fifth Avenue, the large and expensive Manhattan department store, somebody had told her that most aircraft accidents happened on takeoff, and she remembered that comment each time she flew, which was often.

Lucak was sitting in seat 5A, in the business class section on the starboard side of the plane. She was ignoring another piece of advice she had received early in her career. That conventional wisdom said that passengers should fly right behind the wing, because it's the most stable place on the aircraft. If the company wanted her to fly in the more comfortable business class cabin, however, she was not going to give that up to follow some old advice that might or might not have been true in the first place.

She suddenly remembered that she had forgotten to tell her boss an important piece of business, about an order she expected from a large clothing manufacturer in the Dominican Republic, a store that was anxious to carry the valuable and pricy Sak's brand. She picked up the in-seat satellite phone that graced each seat in business class. The rest of the plane's passengers had to share one phone, marked "Public Phone," that was attached to the bulkhead in the economy class section. The fact that the call would cost $10 a minute did not deter her. "The company can afford it," she told herself.

She dialed the number for her boss, Tyler Krebs. He answered and she started to tell him about the new customer and provide contact information when she heard a loud bang behind the wing near her seat, and then a popping sound.

It was not as loud as a big explosion, she thought, but it certainly was enough to bring back her flight jitters.

"Something just hit the plane, exploded near the wing," she blurted out. Her boss responded with "What, what did you say?"

She looked around. The other 18 passengers in business class seemed alert to the noise as well. She decided to ring for the flight attendant. As she did so, she tightened the blue seat belt that was already tight around her waist.

Just then the plane seemed to skid sideways, knocking her into the well-dressed man who was sitting next to her. The plane continued to move sideways, stabilized for a moment and then began to fishtail.

In a panic now, Lucak tightened her seatbelt even more and held on tight. She dropped the phone, no long interested in talking to her boss about a new customer

People in the cabin began to scream and cry. The nose of the plane came up for a few seconds and then dropped once more. She looked out the window. One of the engines was gone from the wing.

Krebs could do nothing as he listened to the final prayers and screams of the dying as he repeatedly called Lucak's name.

"We're dead," Lucak thought, as the nose dropped again, this time for a deadly spiral to the Rockaway peninsula below.

——⚙——

Rob Givens was a happy man. The 45-year-old Givens had just opened a diner on the Rockaway peninsula, the culmination of a life spent working in other people's eateries. It was called the "Rockaway Sunset Diner," and it quickly became the place on the narrow peninsula to go after a night out at the movies or a civic meeting.

Since September, it had also, sadly perhaps, become a place to look at the hole in the New York skyline, directly across the bay, where the World Trade Center had once stood. And, a place for a quick bite to eat after one of the 75 funerals and memorials for those the community who were lost when the two towers fell. The restaurant, after all, was right across busy Beach Channel Drive from Jamaica Bay, with perfect views of both the Manhattan skyline and Kennedy Airport. And, during the summer, the diner was a perfect place to watch the most spectacular sunsets in the state, perhaps the nation.

Rockaway, or at least the west end of the peninsula, was a middle class residential area of well-kept homes and well-manicured lawns, a place where many firefighters, police officers and middle-level workers in the financial world could find community, good schools for their children and a decent place to live within reasonable commuting distance of Manhattan.

Because the west end of Rockaway is directly across Jamaica Bay from Kennedy Airport, many of the planes departing JFK, particularly those departing Runway 31 Left, flew low over the peninsula at regular intervals both day and night. That flight path had been a point of contention between residents and the FAA for years, but most local residents were so accustomed to the planes that they looked up only when the ultra-loud Concorde supersonic transport plane regularly rattled the peninsula four times each day.

In fact, most of the residents knew the Concorde's schedule by heart, two flights out in the morning, two inbound during the afternoon.

That is why Givens looked up when he heard a plane roaring overhead. It was too late for the Air France Concorde departure and still too early for the British Airways version to pass over. Besides, he had heard a Concorde pass over the diner just a few minutes earlier.

He had been serving coffee to a regular customer when he heard the roar.

"Must have added a Concorde to the morning schedule," he said to Ken and Kathy Royster, who were both having the breakfast special at table 27.

Ken, who was seated facing the window that looked towards the bay, looked up.

"Doesn't look like an SST to me," he answered. Looks like a regular jetliner."

Givens turned from pouring the coffee and looked towards the airport.

He was startled by what he saw. The starboard side of the plane, just behind the wing, was engulfed in flame as he watched in horror.

"My God," he fairly yelled, causing the twenty other patrons in the restaurant on this early holiday weekday morning to look in his direction. "It's falling apart."

He and the other patrons looked on in fascination as pieces of the fuselage fell away and then when the tail came off and sailed towards the waters of Jamaica Bay. They stared in a combination of terror and fascination as the now tailless plane, obviously out of control, came straight at the restaurant.

———————•《()》•———————

Timmy Gregory and his wife Gerri were walking their lab, Tahoe, nearby Cross Bay Bridge in Broad Channel. The couple lived on that tiny sliver of land, actually the only inhabitable island in the expanse of Jamaica Bay. Broad Channel connected Rockaway with the rest of the Queens mainland.

They had lived in "The Channel" for two-dozen years and they loved the tight-knit community, a place where you could still leave your doors unlocked at night and where everybody was involved in one community activity or another.

Both of them heard an explosion and the roaring sound at the same time. They looked up.

"Look at that plane, It looks like it's sliding sideways," Tim said to Gerry.

"I think it's on fire," she responded. "Look at the black smoke coming from the other side of the plane."

"That plane is struggling to move in a straight line," Tim thought.

As they watched, the plane went into a flat spin. Then the spin stopped and the nose came up significantly.

"The plane is spinning like a top," Tim exclaimed, more to himself than to Gerry.

As they watched, the tail separated from the body and began to spiral down into the bay.

A moment later, the tailless fuselage of the plane nosed down and spiraled right for the ground.

Then, as they watched in fascination, first one engine and then the other, broke from the plane and dropped towards the land mass of Rockaway.

"Go into the water, go into the water," the couple yelled in unison, but the fireball that they saw erupt from the Rockaway peninsula gave witness to the fact that the plane had crashed into a residential area.

They turned back to head home, Tammy pulling out her cell phone to call 911, but she had barely opened her phone and dialed the emergency number when they heard sirens moving towards them. As they stood transfixed, two fire engines and an ambulance from the Broad Channel Volunteer Fire Department roared past them, on the way to Rockaway. Following them down Cross Bay Boulevard, they could see units of the New York City Fire Department, both from Howard Beach other parts of Queens, as well as a caravan ambulances, both EMS and private, rushing to the scene of the crash.

———————

At about the same time, Charlie Tanner, his wife Joan, and his teenaged daughter, Jennifer, were driving southbound on Flatbush Avenue, just past Floyd Bennett Field and the Barren Island Marina. They were nearly at the southernmost portion of the road, directly across the bay from Rockaway. Charlie Tanner, who was looking for money in the car's ashtray to pay the toll on the Marine Parkway Bridge, was an amateur pilot, who had just earned his pilot's license. He loved to watch the aircraft depart JFK each day. Normally, his family would be driving toward Manhattan at that time of day, but both he and his wife were off for the holiday and his daughter's school was likewise closed. They had gone for breakfast in a diner on Avenue U in Brooklyn and were heading back home to Rockaway.

As they sat at the red light, an aircraft departing the airport caught Tanner's eye. His eye followed it until the light turned green and he moved south towards the bridge. His daughter, however, was still watching the plane.

"Dad," she screamed, causing Tanner to momentarily lose control of his Gallant. "Look, that plane's on fire. He looked up. The plane he had been following a few moments earlier was now on fire, the flames coming from somewhere behind the wing. He watched in fascination as the plane turned towards the Rockaway peninsula. He continued watching until as he drove over the bridge.

Tanner picked up his cellular phone, quickly dialing 911.

The police emergency operator came on.

"Where is your emergency, sir," the disembodied voice asked.

"There is a plane on fire and it looks like it is going down somewhere in Rockaway," he said.

"What is the address or the cross streets of your emergency," the voiced asked.

"I don't know," he yelled, "just get the choppers from Floyd Bennett Field up. They'll know where it came down."

He disconnected when the 911 operator asked him for a name and call back number, thinking that a lot of people were going to die that day that there was nothing he, of anybody else, could do about it.

Tommy Flynn, a retired battalion chief in the New York Fire Department, had ample time to pursue his simple interests, as he was doing now, jogging each morning on the boardwalk from his home on Beach 126th Street, eastward to wherever he got tired on that particular day, usually around Beach 69th Street. That was about six miles out and back. It was a good workout for a 55-year-old man. His retirement also gave him the time to put in countless hours at Ground Zero, as the World Trade Center had come to be called, digging in the ruins, looking for the remains of his brother firefighters.

As always, Tommy ran with his head high, taking in oxygen, getting that good workout.

He was at about Beach 108th Street, heading west towards home, when a muted explosion caused him to look towards the bay. At first, the plane coming towards the peninsula looked normal, although it was lower than planes departing Kennedy usually flew.

Then, he noticed thick black smoke and flames coming from the right side of the plane, just behind the wing. The plane began to oscillate badly, quickly fishtailing from one side to another.

He watched in fascination as a chunk about the size of a door fell from the plane.

Then, without warning, the entire tail section of the plane flew away from the body, soaring down into the waiting water.

Flynn reached for his cellular phone and called 911.

When the emergency operator answered, he quickly asked for a fire dispatcher. He knew that FD would be needed in force in Rockaway, and it would be needed soon.

"This is Tommy Flynn," he said quickly when fire dispatch came on. "Retired Chief in Battalion 47. We have a plane about to crash in Belle Harbor. Get a fifth-alarm response moving to Belle Harbor."

His eyes were riveted on the plane. One engine popped off and then the other. He was a trained observer, and he calculated that the engines landed somewhere around Beach 128 or Beach 129 Street.

He picked up the pace; running now towards the site where he thought the plane would come down, a dense residential area of one and two-family, middle-class homes. He also knew that two schools, PS 114, the local public school and the St. Francis de Sales Parochial School were both in that area, not remembering that it was Veteran's Day, a holiday and both the public and the parochial school would be closed.

Rob Givens and the others in his restaurant on Beach 116 Street also watched the last throes of Flight 587. It passed over the restaurant, trailing smoke and dropping large pieces of debris as it went. The pieces of the plane pelted the restaurant's roof, sounding like a heavy rainstorm.

"Where the hell is the plane's tail." Steve Royster Asked.

"God, it's gone," Rob answered in awe. "There's no way that the plane can stay in the air much longer. I hope it makes it to either the bay or to the ocean. Otherwise, lots of people on the ground are going to die."

———•((•))•———

Bobby Sallow had come out of his girlfriend's ground floor apartment on Beach 130th Street and Beach Channel Drive, right across the drive from the bay. He had been living there with her since he disappeared and died on September 11. He was speaking with her on his smart phone. She was giving him a list of things to do during the day. He was outside looking for the New York Post, which was delivered to the door of their ground-floor apartment each day. The woman who delivered it often flipped the daily newspaper out of her car window at high speed and he often had to look around the flower garden at the side of the house to find it.

He didn't have much to do since the terrorists destroyed his job with Cantor-Fitzgerald at the World Trade Center. Now, he was a man without a job, without a wife and, thanks to his quick thinking and devious mind, without his former identity.

"I guess you really can't go home again, not when you're dead," he mused with a chuckle.

Late for his job that fateful September day, he had watched the first plane hit high on the North Tower, just below the office where he normally would have been sitting at his desk.

Unhappy with his job, with his wife, with his debts and general lack of a future as a bond dealer, he had decided that he could easily be "dead," along with the thousands of others who were surely dead or dying in the building. He had walked away, called his girlfriend and she had readily agreed to help him disappear and start a new life, as long as they were together.

All had been good in the two months since. He was mourned at the memorial services and he was sure his wife would be well taken care of because of his heroic death. What a life, he thought, and he was sure that she would appreciate her new-found wealth more than she did being with him. He was sure he had done the right thing and he was beginning to get on with his new life, his new identity as Ken Beach. He had a job interview the next day with a new restaurant in Rockaway, a low-level job that would not require too close a look at his credentials and would help build his resume for a new future.

He looked towards the bay and Kennedy Airport. It was a beautiful, clear day, much too warm for November, he thought.

He pushed the end button, cutting off his girlfriend's call.

As he watched, a trail of light and smoke lifted from a small boat on the bay and headed upward at a slight angle.

Sallow had been an aviation warfare technician in his four years with the Navy, stationed on an aircraft carrier in the Med. He knew what a missile trajectory looked like. He anticipated the flight of the smoke and saw that a large jetliner was flying right towards it.

"Oh, shit," he said aloud, although nobody was nearby to hear him. "Fucking terrorists."

He quickly pushed the camera icon on his phone and began to tape the missile climbing into the blue sky catching the boat that the missile had come from for a quick second.

He watched in fascination as the smoke from the bay and the plane merged, then he heard a short explosion and saw smoke come from the starboard wing of the plane as well as the tail section.

The plane went into a flat spin and then recovered. The tail fell off and literally flew in circles as it dropped towards the waters of Jamaica Bay. He didn't know what to do. His first thought was to call 911, but he was sure that others would take care of that.

"Everybody had to see that missile go from the bay up to the plane," he thought. "Somebody will report it."

He knew that he couldn't report the missile attack on the jetliner himself. He could never show anybody the tape. He was officially dead in the rubble of the World Trade Center. He had a new life. He couldn't risk all that to report something that was probably seen by hundreds of others in Rockaway. But the thought that nobody else would report it, that he alone had witnessed the attack, still sat heavily on his mind.

"Maybe I'll call the Beachcomber," he thought, "anonymously, of course. Tell them what I saw. Start an investigation going."

Sure that he was right, he picked up his paper and began walking towards the center of the peninsula. He knew that the plane would soon wipe out a portion of Belle Harbor and he wanted to be close on hand to watch, but not too close. You only die once, he thought, and he had already had his turn.

⸺ ◈ ⸺

"We're going in," Shades said to nobody in particular, but his transmission was so garbled that it was not understood up by either TRACON or by ground control. It would take several weeks for sound recording experts to pull his comment from the cockpit voice recorder that was recovered from the wreckage in Belle Harbor.

That was the last that was heard of Flight 587. It was down between Beach 129 and Beach 131 Street along Newport Avenue, but the debris from the plane was spread from Beach 106 Street and Jamaica Bay to Beach 143 Street in Neponsit.

"Look to your south," a private pilot inbound to LaGuardia Airport told TRACON. "There is a plane crashing there."

"An aircraft has just crashed south of the field, somewhere on the tip of Long Island," a JetBlue pilot radioed the JFK tower.

"Affirm a fireball at that location," the JetBlue pilot added.

"Kennedy, are you missing any of your departures," the pilot asked.

"American Flight 587 Heavy," Kennedy responded.

"Kennedy, PD 14," police department search and rescue copter, which was already airborne over its base at Floyd Bennett Field in Brooklyn, and was looking for clearance to fly through the Kennedy pattern, chimed in with a matter-of-fact voice. As second later, that voice changed considerably.

"Holy Shit, a large plane is going down in Belle Harbor," the copter's pilot yelled into his microphone, the tension obvious in his usually calm voice. "Shit, it's going to crash right into the middle of the peninsula. It's breaking up. There's debris in the water in Jamaica Bay and all over the ground. "Clear us to the crash scene," he said to Kennedy control. "Are you missing any aircraft?"

"OK, PD 14, we are trying to figure it out now, sir. We are trying to see if any of our aircraft are missing. Standby."

Central to Aviation 14, can you advise if it was a small plane or a jetliner," the NYPD's central citywide communicator located in northern Brooklyn, asked.

"It's a large jet, and it crashed right into the peninsula, we got smoke and fire everywhere, central. Get FD coming. We're going to need lots of help on this one."

"Uh, Delta 79. It was a heavy jet that went down," a pilot in an arriving aircraft told Kennedy arrival control.

"It was a heavy, sir?" the tower asked the Delta airline pilot.

"Yeah, looked like it."

"PD 6 is going to the crash site."

"PD 6, Kennedy. You are cleared into the Kennedy Class Bravo airspace to, uh, the site, sir. Stay at or below, uh, one thousand feet is approved."

"Kennedy, PD 14. We know the details of what kind of aircraft it was?"

"Kennedy, there is no doubt that it was a heavy and it is down in a residential area."

"Central, Oh-Adam. We have a heavy aircraft down on Beach

1-2-9 crossing Newport. Get a mobilization going," the first police unit to get to the scene radioed to its central command. "This is going to be a bad one."

Two of the last fire alarm boxes left on the peninsula after the final round of citywide budget cuts, were triggered by residents. Box number 1398, located at Beach 127 Street and Newport Avenue was transmitted at 9:17 a.m. Moments later, Box 1441 was transmitted for Bulloch's Gas Station on Beach 129 Street. An airplane engine had just landed inches from its six pumps and then had skidded into its service bay. The engine was on fire.

Ladder 137 and Engine 266, the first apparatus arriving on the scene, transmitted a 10-60, a major emergency response. Shortly thereafter, it signaled a fifth alarm, the highest response call in the FDNY vocabulary.

At the same time, 100 Sergeant called NYPD central dispatch. "Central, this is O-Sergeant. Get a level four mobilization going on my authority. We have a heavy aircraft down in Rockaway."

Within minutes, a large percentage of all of the emergency response vehicles in Queens and in Brooklyn, NYPD, FDNY and EMS, were moving towards Rockaway.

The response to the crash of Flight 587 had begun.

III

Ron Staller was a creature of habit, a trait that came from doing the same job, day after day, year after year, for more than 30 years.

Now, however, those repetitive days had ended three short months before, when the 63-year-old English teacher retired from the city's public school system and bought the local Rockaway newspaper, "The Beachcomber," from its retiring publisher.

Always interested in journalism and enamored with the community in which he had been born and lived in for most of his life, Staller told anybody who would listen that he had "the best job in New York City."

Instead of reporting to the Far Rockaway middle school in which he taught each weekday, a job that had frustrated him daily over the last several years, Staller left home early each day for his newspaper and a job that he had quickly come to love.

Rather small in stature, with thinning white hair and a small mustache that he had cultivated since his wife passed away two years earlier, Staller was a happy man.

His sharp intellect and his desire to find out what was going on – some called it aggressive snooping – had led him to journalism when he was in college and had stayed with him throughout his teaching career, just below the surface, but there nevertheless.

He climbed into his ancient, rusting Chevy Lumina and turned on the ignition. Then, as was his daily habit and part of his new career, he turned on his Radio Shack police scanner and tuned it to 137.50 – the frequency for the two local police precincts, the 100 and the 101.

Listening to the scanner in the car and sometimes even while at home, while writing or watching television had become second nature. He quickly learned the 10-codes used by the NYPD and the scanner had led him to several good stories that later wound up on the front page of his newspaper.

Staller turned left out of his Beach 121st Street driveway and drove towards Rockaway Beach Boulevard, one of the three main east-west roads that transverse the Rockaway peninsula. The area in which Staller lived was called Rockaway Park, a decidedly middle-class mix of 6-story apartment houses, multi-family homes and single-family units. Just four blocks to the west was the community that was called Belle Harbor. There, the homes were mostly one- and two-family, owned by a mix of middle class civil servants, financial district workers and small business owners. Further west still was Neponsit, with its million dollar homes and high-income owners. Then came Riis Park, part of the Gateway National Park and Breezy Point, a gated oceanfront community that catered to the Irish Catholic middle class. No minorities were welcome in Breezy Point, and visitors had to stop at a gatehouse and state their business before being allowed in, something that rankled Staller who had recently written in an editorial, which opined that nobody should have to pass through passport control in their own city.

The aging Staller was thinking about a story he was working on, a story about the owner of a local cell phone store, whose stockbroker son was killed two months before in the World Trade Center. The storeowner, an ex-firefighter, had talked to his son via cell phone after the plane hit the South Tower, telling him to go up to the roof. He was sure that the police helicopters would soon appear to rescue them. Those copters never came, however and that fact took a great toll on the man and his relationship with his family.

A right turn took Staller eastward towards Beach 116th Street, the main shopping area in Rockaway's west end, towards the

Rockaway Sunset Diner, where he stopped each morning, another new habit – hot coffee from September to April, iced coffee from May to August, the daily newspapers and perhaps, a scrambled egg on a roll if he were really hungry and did not have time for an earlier breakfast.

The date being November 12, Staller took hot coffee, the Daily News and the New York Post back to the car. He again headed eastward on Rockaway Beach Boulevard, passing the numerous Irish pubs and second-tier stores that lined the street.

Heading for the newspaper office on Beach 88th Street, Staller loosely listened to "Imus in the Morning" on WFAN while also loosely monitoring the police scanner, which usually was relatively quiet at that time of the morning.

He was at Beach 95 Street heading east, when he heard central dispatch put through a call to the 100 Precinct sector Adam radio motor patrol car. He listened carefully, turning down the Imus Show because he thought he picked up a catch in the voice of the central dispatcher.

"Oh-Adam, check a report of a plane down, Beach 1-2-9 crossing Newport."

He waited for a response, glancing through the rear view mirror to see if there was any smoke coming from the area directly behind him. He knew well from even two months experience not to react to the first call, that the information was often wrong or a prank on the part of somebody with nothing better to do.

The thought of a plane down in that crowded community, even a small plane, was chilling, however, and Staller started to look for a place to turn around. He involuntarily held his breath while waiting for some confirmation on the part of the responding patrol car.

That confirmation came within seconds.

"Central, 100 Adam," the radio crackled. "We have a heavy aircraft down on Newport Avenue, crossing 1-2-9 to 1-3-1. Get a mobilization going!"

Staller's pulse quickened. He could hear the tension in the voice of the anonymous cop making the call. In addition, and perhaps more importantly, his police officer son lived on the beach block of Beach 129th Street.

He quickly swung into Beach 94th Street, made a screeching turn and headed west. In a block or two, he could see the dark, dense smoke rising above the buildings that lined the street. There was only one question in his mind: Was the smoke on the ocean side of Rockaway Beach Boulevard, where his son lived? Or, was it on the bay side of the boulevard?

He speeded up, passing red lights, honking his horn to warn other drivers. Even though he was still developing the "get the story first" instinct, he had to find out if his son was OK before he did anything else. Behind him, he could hear the cacophony of sirens that marked the beginning of the hundreds of emergency vehicles rushing towards Rockaway.

———— ≈»《●》«≈ ————

Cliff Mapes was an ironworker, but he had not worked much at constructing buildings for the past two months. He was too busy each day digging in the ruins of the World Trade Center, looking for his brother, Steve, a firefighter with Ladder 25, whose body had yet to be found. He was working the night tour this week, so he was at home with his wife, Toni, a public school teacher at the local elementary school, who had the day off for Veteran's Day. The couple's three children were all away at college, so they could enjoy a quiet breakfast for two with no reason or rush and no place to go. There were not many days that they had that luxury.

They were drinking coffee in their Beach 129th Street home, talking about Ground Zero when the heard a loud noise.

"The Concorde must be off schedule," Toni said with a laugh.

"It's too loud even for the Concorde," Cliff answered.

They heard a quick popping sound and then a loud crash.

"Sounds like a truck hit a house," Cliff said as ran to the door and looked up and down Beach 129th Street. The St. Francis de

Sales Church and its parochial school, diagonally across the street looked quiet. The school was closed for the holiday, but the church was celebrating a mass for veterans. He looked quickly in the other direction, towards the bay. He saw black smoke coming from the small strip of stores on the next block.

"Call 911," he yelled to Toni. "It looks like the gas station is on fire. Tell them it's at Bulloch's Gas Station. A gas truck must have exploded."

Toni ran to the phone.

Cliff looked around for a jacket. Steve's spare set of turnout gear and helmet hung from a hook outside the closet. Somehow, they could not get up the energy to put it in storage, especially with his remains still not identified. He quickly pulled on his dead brother's gear and ran towards the fire.

———

Jimmy Bechtold heard the same pop, the same crash that Mapes heard. He lived closer to the gas station. In fact, he lived right across the street.

Neither emergencies nor catastrophic incidents were anything new to Bechtold. He had been a police officer in his youth before rolling over to the fire department. He had done his 30 years with FD and retired as a captain. He had seen his share of fire, his share of death and destruction.

He could still deeply feel death all around him. His two firefighter sons had been in the World Trade Center. Bill, who worked at Rescue One, had managed to crawl out of the rubble of Tower Two. They had not yet found Colin's body. The two spent hours most days searching the rubble pile for a piece of Collin.

Bechtold looked out his living room window. He could not believe his eyes. What looked to him to be a small truck was sitting in the gas station across the street. It was aflame and it was threatening the nearby pumps.

Bechtold ran from his house towards the fire. He turned back and grabbed the long garden hose attached to a faucet on the front of his house. He turned on the water and carried the nozzle across the narrow street towards the roaring, flames, realizing as he got closer that the burning object was not a truck, but a large aircraft engine.

Two of station's employees were also fighting the fire, using a hose from the station's repair bay. They were making little headway with the fuel-fed fire, however.

Bechtold joined them, trying to sweep the fire away from the engine and into the street with well-aimed streams of water.

He looked up and saw that there was even more smoke now coming from an area about two blocks away, further west and a block south, on Newport Avenue. His restaurant, "The Lighthouse," was on the north side of Newport Avenue at Beach 130 Street. He had owned it for twenty years, and he silently hoped that it was still there. He was a firefighter first and a restaurant owner second, and he could not leave the gas station until this fire was out. Then, he would look at his restaurant. He knew that he would not have to look far to find all the fire that he and his brother firefighters could handle.

He saw a firefighter running towards him and wondered where his fire engine was. They could use an engine to knock down the fire. Then he saw that the firefighter was Cliff Mapes, a frequent customer at The Lighthouse bar and another family member of a 911 victim.

Cliff grabbed a second hose from the repair bay and the three hoses working together began to make a dent on the engine fire.

"Where the hell did this come from," Mapes asked nobody in particular. "Did you see the plane pass over?"

"Look over there," Bechtold shrugged his shoulders and head to the left. "I think that the rest of the plane is over there."

Mapes looked towards Newport Avenue.

The smoke was so thick that it looked as if the tops of the houses were missing. Perhaps they were.

Staller parked his Lumina on Beach Channel Drive and Beach 129th Street about three blocks from the fire scene and his son's apartment. He could see now that the fire was just north of the boulevard and towards the bay, perhaps on either Cronston or Newport Avenues. He also knew that if he parked too close to the roaring fire, the emergency responders, who surely were on the way to the conflagration, would probably block him in. He had learned the hard way not to park too close to a fire or other emergency just two weeks before, when his car got blocked in by fire apparatus and police cars for several hours after a three-alarm fire.

He grabbed both his new digital camera and the Canon EOS that used traditional film. He was glad that he kept his equipment and extra rolls of film packed in the trunk of his car. He put on his shooting vest, built more hunting in Africa than for camera lenses and film, and packed the myriad of pockets with rolls of film and floppy disks that acted as film media for his digital Sony Mavica.

Fire trucks, ambulances and police emergency cars began to roar past him on Beach Channel Drive, heading further west. He wondered where the center of the fire was, where the plane had come down.

"If that thing came down at a shallow angle, we've lost half the neighborhood," he thought.

The last thing he did was to shove his scanner, now tuned to the NYPD citywide emergency services frequency into the top pocket. He had a feeling that it would provide the clues as to which way to go.

First, however, he had to check to make sure that his son, Ken, was OK.

After walking a block south towards the ocean, Staller saw that four men, a firefighter and three civilians were fighting the fire in what looked to him to be a small car in the neighborhood gas station.

There was little that he could do to help them, so Staller stopped, grabbed his digital camera and began to shoot pictures of the men fighting the fire.

His photos would be on the AP wire and around the world before the day was out.

Staller continued on. As he passed Newport Avenue, he could see men in civilian clothes fighting numerous fires, joining uniformed firefighters and their rigs. It was strange to see civilians pulling hose and directing the stream of water at the fires, but many of them seemed to know what they were doing. Even stranger to Staller was the sight of police officers assisting the firefighters in getting the hose off the trucks and the water onto the fires. There was a traditional animosity between the two uniformed services that seemed to have been transcended by the emergency.

It looked to Staller as if dozens of homes were on fire. Others were gone completely. Pieces of aircraft, mixed with pieces of the destroyed homes, were all over the street, all over the well-kept lawns of the single-family homes. For a number of those homes, only the lawns were left.

He continued up the block, arriving at his son's apartment in a neat two-family home only three houses from the beach. He rang the bell, but nobody answered.

Staller had the keys to his son's apartment because he often walked Rusti, his son's mutt, when he was on some extended duty. His son, Ken was gone, but the house was safe and he had to assume that he was safe as well.

Just at that minute, his son, 35-year-old NYPD Sergeant Ken Staller was at the United Nations building on the east side of Manhattan leading a planning session on how to keep terrorists out of the building during the big General Assembly that was to be held the following week. That assembly would draw most of the world's leaders to New York City and everybody was nervous about the possibility of another terrorist attack.

Like his father, Staller was short of stature, about 5 feet, nine inches tall, with a thin, wiry body. His dirty blonde hair was kept high and tight and he had maintained a crew cut since he played baseball at Queens College. He looked like what he was, an NYPD cop. He walked the walk and talked the talk and it was obvious to those city dwellers who met with him that he was "on the job."

He had walked beats in South Jamaica and, after his promotion to sergeant, in lower Manhattan. He had his share of arrests and his share of gun runs. Like many cops, Staller had been married for a short time, but his time away from home and his experiences on the job had somehow changed him. His wife had filed for divorce after four years, telling him that he was no longer the man she married and she no longer wanted to share her husband with the job. Staller considered it an occupational hazard.

Now, Staller was part of a planning unit called the "Tactical Crowd Control Unit." Everybody on the job called it the TCCU. His unit planned for and controlled major events. That was a great job when the major event was a World Series game at Yankee Stadium., but not such a great job when it meant the major event was the "Million Man March," a police involved shooting or, like today, the visit of 40 world leaders to the United Nations.

Staller was talking to his boss, the Deputy Chief in charge of the UN detail when the citywide radio that he always kept tucked in his back pocket crackled.

"Emergency Service Trucks seven, eight, nine and ten, we have a level four mobilization at Beach 129 Street and Newport Avenue in the confines of the 100 Precinct for a heavy aircraft down at that location. Mobilization point is 131 and Newport."

Staller was stunned.

"Chief, I've got to go," he said, more urgently than he had intended.

"What do you mean, go, we have a detail here to run," the chief responded somewhat miffed by his subordinate.

"An airplane just dropped on my house," he said, turning up his department radio so the chief could hear the urgent calls of first responders for assistance.

The chief's jaw dropped, but he said nothing. Both he and Staller had been in the World Trade Center just two months earlier, trying to figure out why the department radios seemed to be out of order. The two men had walked out of the south tower and down West Street when the building came down behind them, leaving them under a fire truck and covered with white powder. They had seen each other often in the intervening weeks as both worked "the pile," what was left of the two massive buildings brought down by terrorists.

The chief knew that Staller had to get to Rockaway not only because it was his home, but because his job demanded that he be at high-profile crime scenes, as well as high-profile disasters such as the plane crash. His expertise would be needed more in Rockaway than in Manhattan at that particular moment in time.

Staller rushed to his department car and sped, lights and sirens through the Midtown Tunnel onto The Long Island Expressway, getting off the impacted road at the first exit and south into Cross Bay Boulevard heading for Rockaway.

IV

When Ron Staller reached the corner of Beach 130th Street and Newport Avenue, he had difficulty in processing the scene. His neighborhood was literally burning down around him, fire and destruction surrounding him on three sides.

Thick, black smoke was everywhere. Police and fire units from several jurisdictions roared into the scene. People yelled, civilians ran from their homes, some still in the pajamas and robes. Most were shoeless.

He stood on the corner of Beach 131st Street and Newport Avenue, in front of the Lighthouse restaurant, and watched the houses right across Beach 131st Street burn. Diagonally to his right, across Newport Avenue, the houses on both sides of the corner of Beach 131 Street were on fire. The smoke and flames from Beach 131 south of Newport were so heavy that it looked like the area was cloaked in a deep fog.

Bodies, many still strapped into their airplane seats lay on the ground. Parts of the aircraft were everywhere.

Each five-man fire truck quickly drew twenty additional civilian and off-duty volunteers, as civilians, police officers, off-duty fire-fighters and even restaurant workers pulled hose from trucks, attached hose to the hydrants and generally assisted the professional firefighters any way they could.

At least a dozen homes were burning. The four homes on the corner of Beach 131st and Newport were completely gone, now only shells. An engine had fallen into the backyard of a one-family home on Beach 128th Street, just north of Newport Avenue, quickly turning the home into an inferno. Two houses down, part a wing stood in a backyard, leaning against a tree as if it had been set there by a mad landscape artist.

Staller began shooting pictures, alternating the digital and film cameras. As quickly as he could, he exchanged floppy disks in his digital and film rolls in his film camera, shooting hundreds of images as quickly as he could reload. He moved from corner to corner, from street to street in a two-block square area, recording the bravery and the heartache.

He recognized many of the men fighting the fire. Some were local firefighters, others, people he knew from the community. Volunteer fire units from Broad Channel, Breezy Point and Point Breeze rolled in and added their apparatus to the scene. The first job seemed to be getting the fires out, but firefighters and police officers were already beginning to look for survivors in the homes and to gather the bodies of those who were on the plane. As quickly as fires were extinguished, firefighters and cops searched the property for survivors in need of medical attention. It quickly became apparent that this was a recovery effort rather than a search and rescue operation. There were no survivors either on the plane of in the homes that were destroyed by the crash and raging fire.

The large parking area in the rear of the Lighthouse became a triage area and a mobilization point for the dozens of ambulances that rushed to the scene. The EMT's and drivers assigned to those rigs just stood and waited. There were no injured, except for a few firefighters who suffered from smoke inhalation.

Like the scene at the World Trade Center, where most of the same first responders had been just two months and a day before, there was nobody to work on, nobody to rush to local hospitals.

Staller walked towards a fire engine and saw a couple of the Broad Channel Volunteers moving through what was once a home and was now a smoldering wreck. He had written a front-page story about four of the volies who had been buried in the rubble of the

Trade Center when it came down. The four volunteers, one of whom had been hit so hard in the back by the debris from the falling building that his teeth had literally been knocked from his mouth and his boots from his feet, were looking for the bodies of those who lived in the house. Across the street from them, city firefighters tagged the bodies of those who died on the plane.

Staller had interviewed the four men just six weeks before for a prize-winning series of stories entitled, "Is Anybody Out There Still Alive," the question one of them had asked to nobody in particular while he was buried in and blinded by the white dust that was all that remained of the South Tower. The four were pulled from under their crushed ambulance and taken to New Jersey by police launch. Three of them wound up in Jersey hospitals, but they were here, back on duty.

Staller thought of questioning them for this story as well, but they were busy working, and he knew how to reach them. He would have plenty of time later on to speak with them. He shot some photos of them working in the debris pile and then moved on. Concentrating on shooting a picture of some civilians digging in the steaming rubble of what was once a home, Staller almost tripped on what he thought was a piece of concrete. He looked at it closely and then picked it up. It was hot to the touch, scorched on the edges and smooth.

"Must be a piece of the wreckage from the aircraft," he thought to himself, absently putting it into the pocket of his shooting vest. He would give it to the police later on, he decided.

He saw two familiar figures digging through the rubble of a house that had been destroyed. Both Cliff Mapes and Jimmy Bechtold had seen been putting out the fire in the gas station. Now, they were on their knees, digging at a rubble pile, looking for both the survivors and the dead. He knew them both well. Cliff's wife worked at a nearby school, and his firefighter brother had been lost at the Trade Center. Jimmy was the owner of the Lighthouse. An ex-firefighter, his son had been lost in the Trade Center as well.

Both had spent days digging in the rubble pile for their relatives at Ground Zero. Neither had been found. Now they were digging much closer to home for more recent victims. Were they victims of terrorism just like their relatives. Perhaps. Perhaps not.

Then the question struck him full-bodied for the first time.

"Was the crash of AA 587 an accident or a terrorist act?" he asked himself. He wanted to think that it was an accident, but the idea that it was a terrorist bomber or, perhaps another case of hijackers trying to take over an aircraft that failed, as had the one in Pennsylvania a two months before.

As if to accentuate the thought, a screaming roar hit him like a hammer. Two U.S Air Force F-15 Strike Eagles roared low overhead. Everybody, including those actively fighting fires or digging for survivors, looked up. The Air Force fighters passed out of sight, replaced by a single Navy F-14 Tomcat that circled the area for a few minutes and then departed with a deafening roar as the plane went to afterburner to return to its carrier, just offshore.

Staller could see that the same thought that he had only moments before was now on everybody's mind.

As he walked the fire scene, he heard the same comments over and over again.

"I heard that it was a terrorist bomb."

"Some guy over there said that he saw a missile strike the plane just before it came down. I heard that it was fired by one of those jets because the airliner had been hijacked and was heading for the Empire State Building."

"I heard that some Muslims tried to take over the plane and the passengers and crew resisted, and it came down in Rockaway."

"I heard that the plane was brought down in Rockaway as retaliation for a comment a Rockaway firefighter made on the telethon on TV last week."

Staller was not convinced. Facts were any reporter's stock in trade and he was not going to print anything about the cause of the accident until he had the hard facts.

While his father shot pictures of the crash scene, NYPD Sergeant Staller finally got to the crash scene. Staller wore his regular working attire, a dark blue shirt with NYPD across the back, a sergeant's badge embodied on the front with his name and badge number, cargo pants with large pockets on each side, his duty belt and Glock nine-millimeter automatic and his raid jacket with the sergeant's stripes on the sleeve and the large "NYPD – TCCU" on the back.

He parked his department car on Beach 127th Street and jogged over to the scene. He saw the yellow crime tape that now surrounded the scene and noticed that dozens of reporters and camerapersons were standing behind the tape, struggling for position, trying to film the scene a few blocks away. He recognized some of the television reporters, many doing stand-ups in front of the camera, with their backs to the inferno.

He took a quick survey of the area, looking for his father, sure that he had to be somewhere around the crash scene.

"I just hope he's keeping himself out of trouble," he thought. He knew his dad was not going to obey the official restrictions and was probably more concerned with getting the story and the photos than with standing a few blocks away with the other journalists.

He took out his cell phone and hit the autodial number for his father's phone.

His father answered quickly and he could hear sirens and loud voices in the vicinity. He knew for sure that his father was somewhere inside the "frozen zone" that had been established to keep everybody but responders and investigators out of the area.

"Hello, Ron Staller," his father answered.

"Are you OK. Where are you?" his son asked.

"I was expecting to hear from you sooner or later. I'm at 130 and Newport, shooting photos," his father answered. "Where are you? Are you coming to the scene?"

"I'm at the other end, at 133 and Newport, heading into the crime scene," his son said. "You're in the frozen zone and they'll probably try and throw you out, move you back to the church. Stay out of trouble and I'll try and work my way over to you."

He closed the flip phone and moved under the yellow crime scene tape.

One of the first people that Sergeant Staller saw as he ducked under the yellow tape was Ed Lopat, a local agent with the National Transportation Safety Board, stationed at the FAA headquarters building at JFK Airport. Staller had worked with Lopat the previous year, when his NYPD unit ran a series of emergency drills, setting up a scenario where a transport plane came down in the middle of Jamaica bay. An old aircraft fuselage was dumped into the bay off the Rockaway shoreline and first responders, including police and fire scuba divers and others from Coast Guard and the Parks Police had to go in to retrieve the survivors of the crash. The site they used was about 100 yards from where the tail of AA 587 landed in the bay. Staller wished that this plane had done its duty and gone into the bay rather than into the street where he lived.

Lopat and a few others with "NTSB" in large letters on the back of their raid jackets were picking up small pieces of debris. Each of them had a large bag and a number of small bags. When any of them recovered a piece of the aircraft, he or she would photograph the debris in situ, tag the item with the time, date and location, and put it into a small baggie and then into the larger bag.

Staller walked up to Lopat.

"What have you got," Staller asked. That question was a shorthand method used by police for asking for some information that would help them understand what had happened — information that he could pass on to his boss.

"Not much, so far," Lopat responded. He knew Staller and respected his professionalism. He also knew that Staller worked for the NYPD's Chief of the Department, and he knew that whatever he said would soon be repeated to the top brass at the department.

"So, far, looks like an accident, but it's really too early to tell" Lopat added. "Luckily, the plane came down in a tight spiral. If it had come in on a flat trajectory, it would have wiped out half of the neighborhood killed dozens of locals."

"This one is going to be a bitch," he added. "The engines

separated before the plane hit and so did the tail. We can't seem to find the tail."

Lopat mused that he hoped it was an accident, but he was not sure. For one thing, there was too much debris outside of the crash site. For another, he was hearing stories that a number of locals had seen the plane on fire while it was still in the air.

The New York State governor, however, had already gone on record, calling it an accident rather than a crime, and had officially moved the investigation from the NYPD and FBI to the civilian NTSB.

"The aviation community can't take another terrorist hit like 911 or the shoe-bomber," Staller said, almost to himself. "If the public loses confidence in the industry to keep its planes in the air, the trains are going to be awfully crowded during the coming holiday season."

Lopat told Staller about the governor's declaration.

Looking around, Staller wondered why so many FBI agents were involved in picking through the wreckage and talking to people at the scene if the crash had already been declared an accident. That job should have fallen to the NTSB and the FBI should have left the scene to that agency.

Staller worried about the fact that government officials were already calling it an accident, even before the investigation had really begun. In his mind, it was much too early in the investigation to make that call, unless they knew something that he didn't know. He was skeptical of the feds and, like most cops, did not believe in coincidences. Planes used by terrorists to bring down the World Trade Center and then, two months later, another plane crashes into Rockaway. Coincidence or another threat? He hoped he could help find out, even though such an investigation did not fit into his job description. This was just too close to home to be ignored.

Staller thanked Lopat and moved on. His radio, which was a constant source of noise and messages under the best of conditions, was overwhelmed by the orders and information flying around the citywide net today.

He wanted to find the other members of his team, so he picked the radio up to his lips. He called the NYPD's central radio command in Brooklyn.

"TCCU Sergeant, Central, can you raise TCCU CO?"

Before central could answer, Staller heard a harbor unit launch, Harbor Adam, calling central.

"Harbor Adam, Central, can you reach out to the Coast Guard? We have the tail of the aircraft in tow at Beach 108 Street, about 100 yards off shore, nearby the water treatment plant."

"10-4 Adam, we'll make the call by landline," the central dispatcher answered quickly. "All other units 10-6 for a moment please."

Staller knew that the dispatcher had gone offline to make the important call. He waited before trying to reach his team one more time.

Most of the fires were now out. What was left of a half-dozen homes stood smoldering, with bodies still locked in their seats and aircraft wreckage all over the property where those houses once stood. He walked over to the mobile command post that had been set up on the playground of St. Francis de Sales Church on Beach 129th Street and Rockaway Beach Boulevard, right down the block from his house. One of his jobs was training other cops who ran the command post setup, so he knew most of the people inside.

"Any idea on causalities," he asked a uniformed officer sitting at a telephone switchboard inside the large mobile command post.

"Anywhere from none to a dozen so far, Sarge," he answered. "That's if you don't count those on the plane. We have no numbers so far, but it looks like a couple of hundred total at least, even if the number on the ground is small."

Staller walked out of the command post and back to the scene.

"The tail is in the bay about a mile away," he thought to himself, "one engine is on Beach 128th, the other on Beach 129th. There are pieces of the aircraft scattered from Beach 116th Street to the end of the peninsula. What the hell happened?"

That was precisely the question that was on hundreds of minds that afternoon.

Ron Staller was walking back towards the Lighthouse when a police sergeant who he knew from the local precinct stopped him.

"Ron, are you supposed to be in this area," the sergeant asked. "You know that all the press is over near St. Francis. How did you get inside the yellow tape?

Staller laughed. "I was here long before they set the frozen zone, Sarge. "I got what I need, so I'll go quietly.

"We've set up a press area the other side of Beach 128th and Newport," he told Staller. The press is being asked to stay back there. We will be holding a press conference in about a half hour in the St. Francis playground. This area has been declared a crime scene, so make your way out. Take it as slow as you want."

"Sorry," he added with a smile that made it clear that he wasn't sorry at all, wondering again whether or not the installation of a crime scene made the crash a terrorist act. He decided that it was just another bureaucratic snafu.

Staller walked back to his car on Beach 129th and Beach Channel Drive. He had to back out of the one-way street in order to head back to his office. He did not need the press conference. Every media outlet in the United States would cover the conference, but this was his beat and he knew his way around without the help of the authorities who would hold the press conference. He was sure he could watch it on the television set that was always on and tuned to NY1 news or CNN in his office when he got back there in ten minutes or so.

As he drove eastward on Beach Channel Drive, heading for the one-hour photo shop that developed his film, he saw a line of fire apparatus and ambulances still heading for the scene in the other direction. Interspersed with the emergency vehicles were dozens of satellite trucks that provided the transmission facilities and support for the three major networks as well as all of the local stations.

The world was about to drop in on his relatively-quiet peninsula, and Staller was not all sure that he was going to like the change at all.

———————×((○))×———————

Tommy Lewis drove an ambulance for a private service, Hunter Ambulance. He had not been dispatched to the fire scene, but had no trouble getting past the checkpoints the police had now set up for several blocks in each direction surrounding the crash site. Tommy just wanted to see "what was shaking," and he quickly realized that there were no survivors, no work for him to do here.

He was driving north on Beach 128th Street when he saw a piece of metal standing against a tree in a side yard. It looked vaguely like part of an airplane wing, so he stopped and took a look. Nobody else seemed to be around, although the street was lined with emergency vehicles. He walked into the yard and looked at the large, flat piece of metal that looked like a piece of an airplane. He picked it up. It was black and charred and still slightly hot to the touch.

"This baby's been in an explosion," he said to himself looking at the black residue that coated the piece of metal.

On a whim, he turned around and carried it to his ambulance.

He had a plan. He would put the piece of metal into his ambulance and stop at his Wavecrest Gardens apartment before checking back in with the company at its Inwood base. Maybe he could find a way to make some cash from the piece of blackened, twisted wreckage.

———————×((○))×———————

Sarah Lefkowitz heard the crash when flight 587 hit only five blocks west of where she lived, on the beach block of Beach 126 Street. She heard the screaming sirens of the responding emergency vehicles.

———

She ran into the street to see what was going on, throwing her coat over her shoulders as she ran. The smoke was thick and choking. She stepped on something hard and looked down. It was a green-colored seat belt, the kind used in cars. Or, she thought, in airplanes. She picked the seatbelt up and stuffed it into her coat pocket. Then she went back inside to call her sister in Arizona to tell her what was going on nearby her Rockaway home.

———◆———

The fires were finally out and the body count begun. Only a few residents of the homes in the crash area were unaccounted for, and the great majority of them would be quickly found.

First responders and investigators were busy dealing with the hundreds of bodies of flight 587's passengers and crew, many of whom were still strapped into their seats with tough, wide blue seatbelts, sitting in the rubble where a two-story family home once stood.

Ed Lopat had called in the NTSB's "Go Team," a group of experts in discrete areas of aircraft expertise that was always ready to leave for an accident scene at a moment's notice. Lopat surveyed the scene in front of him and understood instinctively that, despite the low death toll on the ground, this was going to be one of the worst.

Most of the fire apparatus and ambulances had already left the scene. This was no longer a rescue effort, but a recovery. That fact was reinforced when the vans from the city's medical examiner began to arrive.

It was clear that nobody on the A300 had survived, not passengers nor crew. It was also clear that whoever was on that plot of land when the Airbus augured in was no longer alive.

He was deep in his own thoughts when Ken Staller walked up behind him.

"Not very good, is it?" the sergeant asked.

"Not good at all," Lopat answered.

"Have you found the CVR or FDR yet," referring to the "black boxes" that would show the last minutes of the life of Flight 587.

"Still looking. We'll find them. They couldn't have gone far. At least this is better than trying to find the black boxes in 500 feet of water. In this case, even though they're located near the tail and the tail is in the bay, I think that we'll find them somewhere nearby the fuselage here on land."

Both the Cockpit Voice Recorder and the Flight Data Recorder, which were really red, were important to the coming investigation and Lopat would have liked to have them secured before the "Go Team" arrived.

Lopat had detailed two engine companies to search around the wreckage of the rear of the plane to look for the FDR and CVR. So far, however, the 10 firefighters had no luck.

"What do you think, accident or something else," Staller asked.

"All I know so far is that a plane can't fly without a tail. Your harbor unit found the tail about a mile away, floating in the bay. The major question is going to be, why did the tail separate from the fuselage? The tail may be the key piece of evidence that completes the puzzle.

Lopat and Staller walked together towards the site where fire-fighters, police officers and others were picking up bodies and body parts and placing them in slick, black body bags. Those bags would then be removed to a hangar in Floyd Bennett Field and eventually to the city's morgue, where the medical examiner and his assistants would document the cause of death and search for the identification of the victim."

"How many on the ground," Lopat asked.

"We don't know yet. Maybe a dozen, probably less."

"Damned lucky. Almost a miracle," Lopat said. "A heavy like this comes down in a tight neighborhood like this one and kills only a dozen. God-damned miracle."

"There are five for sure," Staller added. "A man in that house over there, a woman and her son in that house over here. We just got word that the daughter was playing basketball at the church on

1-2-9. We thought at first that she was home as well. The house that used to stand where all the bodies are being picked up, we're not sure. One woman lived there alone. We think that she was out, maybe at work at a local doctor's office, but we're still checking."

Lopat just shook his head to show that he understood the difficulty of checking in this kind of situation, where the destruction was over a relatively small area, but you couldn't be sure who was home and who wasn't.

Staller and Lopat watched the body retrieval in silence. Both men had spent time at Ground Zero, the growing pit where the World Trade Center buildings had stood. They both had enough of body retrieval for a lifetime. Here they were, however, only two months and a day later, at it again.

One of those picking up bodies was Tommy Flynn. Though he was retired, his credentials got him through the police lines. He wanted to help. He needed to help, but his mind was more on the scene he had seen in the air over Rockaway more than on what he was doing.

He spotted a man in a raid jacket speaking with a police sergeant. When the man turned, he saw the large, yellow "NTSB" on the back of his jacket.

Flynn made a decision. He stopped what he was doing and walked up to the man.

"Hey, he said. My name is Tom Flynn, and I'm a retired FD battalion chief. I saw the plane explode in the air before it crashed."

Lopat was taken aback. Staller, who was watching the exchange, stayed out of the discussion. This was between the firefighter and Lopat.

"You're sure of that," Lopat asked.

"Sure as I am of anything," Flynn answered. "I was on the job for 30 years. I know a fire and smoke when I see them."

Lopat took a notebook from his rear pocket.

"Give me your name, address and telephone number. There will be a witness unit with the Go Team. I'll have them contact you sometime in the next few days."

"Can't you take my statement, save some time?"

"Not my job. The team would only have to go over it with you all over again. It will only be a few days."

Flynn gave Lopat his information and walked away, shaking his head.

Staller knew of Flynn, had seen him at many of the local firefighter funerals that both had attended since September 11.

"Seems like a credible witness to me," Staller said. "Firefighter, trained observer. Doesn't panic when he's seen something out of the ordinary."

Lopat shook his head. "Most eyewitnesses believe what they think they have seen, but are relatively as useless as shit," he answered. "Might be right, probably wrong, I'll let the investigation team sort that out."

His words were interrupted by a shout from a firefighter bending over the wreckage about 200 feet away.

The firefighter triumphantly held up a red rectangular object with wires coming from its side.

"Looks like we got the CVR," Lopat said. He began to walk towards the firefighter to retrieve the box.

Staller decided to head back to the temporary headquarters vehicle parked in the playground across from St. Francis de Sales Church. He wanted badly to go home, which was just up the block. He knew, however, that he had lots to do before he could go home that night.

Rob Givens decided to climb the ladder that ran from the attic of his diner to the roof. As the doomed plane flew over his restaurant in the morning, he and his customers could hear debris raining on the roof, and it was time to check it out and see if there were any damage to his roof or the air conditioning units that sat above the restaurant.

He climbed through a trap door and scanned the roof, looking for structural damage, hoping he would find none. The last thing he needed was for the building's department to close him down while repairs were made.

There were small and medium pieces of metal and charred padding all over the roof, although it did not look like there was any structural damage. He was surprised that the NTSB did not want to look at the roof while it was still light. Perhaps tomorrow, he thought. He pulled out his camera and took some photos of the debris and then gathered up some of the smaller pieces of charred debris and put it in a large black garbage bag, which he took with him when he climbed back down through the trap door. He would save it for investigators if they wanted it. If not, he would put it out with the trash on Monday. He could not believe that the FBI or the NTSB or somebody wouldn't want the debris he found on the roof.

———((●))———

At the same time that Ken Staller was entering the temporary headquarters, his father was fending off dozens of phone calls from all over the world.

Back at the Beachcomber office, the phones were literally ringing off the hook.

"Ron, BBC London on three," Carol, the receptionist, already harried from dozens of similar calls, yelled out.

Staller picked up the phone and pushed the "three" button.

"Mr. Staller, this is John Langford, BBC Service, in London. I understand that you just came back from the crash site," the decidedly British voice asked.

"Yes, that's true," Staller said.

"We'd like to do a quick, on-air interview if we could, the voice said,

"Sure, why not?"

"Stand by, sir, we'll be going to you in 10-9-8-7-6."

Staller could hear the British announcer doing an introduction, telling that he was the editor of a weekly paper nearby the crash site in Belle Harbor.

"5-4-3-2-1. We have with us on the line, Ron Staller, who is the editor of the local newspaper in Belle Harbor, where today an airliner crashed into a residential neighborhood. Mr. Staller, can you tell us what the scene looked like?"

Staller answered the question and waited for the next.

"Can you speculate for us what caused the crash, Mr. Staller?"

That was the Sixty-four dollar question, Staller thought. Did he want to speculate?

"I think it was an accident that the tail somehow separated from the plane" he answered. He thought of Tommy Flynn. "There are many, however, who say that they saw the plane on fire, that there was some sort of explosion before the plane fell."

"Then you can't rule out some sort of terrorism, can you?"

"No, I can't," Staller answered quietly.

The interview ended, but others came quickly on its heels.

BBC, Melbourne, Italy, several papers in the western part of the United States. The Boston Globe, the Los Angeles Times, Newsday, Newsweek,

"Ron, AP on four."

He picked up the phone and hit the button.

"Ron Staller."

"Ron, this is Tom Folkes, a photo editor with the associated press. I understand that you got some good digital pictures of the crash scene today. We'd like to buy all you have."

Staller was not sure how they associated press knew about his pictures, but it was a compliment that they wanted them.

"Sure, why not. We're really not competitors, after all," Staller laughed.

"Great, we'll pay you $500 a picture for any we use. How does that sound?"

"Fine. What's your e-mail address? I'll send you a couple of the best digital photos I have. I don't have the film developed yet."

Folkes gave Staller his e-mail address and hung up. Staller had been playing with Photoshop, opening up some of his disks, picking out the best pictures and saving them in a computer file he had slugged simply "AA587."

He sent a dozen of the best to Folkes on the paper's DSL line, hoping that they would buy a couple, not just for the money, but for the byline, "Photo by Ron Staller – AP."

"Ron, NBC, Today Show on three."

He picked up the phone once again.

"Ron Staller."

"Mr. Staller, this is Tammy Thompson a field producer with the Today Show. Matt Lauer and his crew are going to be in Rockaway early tomorrow morning doing a remote from the crash scene and we'd like to do a live interview with you on our program. Staller hoped that the interviewer would be Katy Couric rather than Matt Lauer, but he'd take either.

Sure," he answered. "Sounds great."

"I need one promise," Thompson said. "You won't do any other morning shows tomorrow. We need an exclusive to do this."

"I've made no other promises. That's OK with me," Staller answered, in a kind of daze that network television usually brings to the initiated.

"Talk to you later, then," Thompson said, breaking the connection.

This was going to be a long night.

———— ‹‹◊›› ————

Shafiq was angry. Omar should have known that all other flights would be postponed right after 587 went down, just as they were on 9/11.

"Damn it," he said aloud, drawing the looks of the other passengers of the London-bound aircraft that was supposed to take off 20 minutes before. Instead, all of the passengers had been removed from the plane and told to wait in the British Airways terminal at JFK.

Shafiq went to a bank of telephones and waited his turn at a phone. When it was his turn, he quickly dialed a number from memory.

A male voice answered.

"6-4-8-7," the voice said.

"I am still at Kennedy," Shafiq replied. "All flights are grounded. They are treating the crash as a terrorist act."

The voice at the other end chuckled.

"Don't laugh. I should have been on the way home by now. Now I am stuck her for another day and they may be looking for me."

"Just be calm, and nothing will happen. You have your rights, and they will not bother you," the voice, which he was sure was Omar, said. "You will be home tomorrow. Judging from the television news, nobody has reported seeing anything suspicious about the plane before its demise. You are in the clear. We do have other problems, however."

"What happened?"

"Kabul fell to the Northern Alliance today," the voice said. "Our brothers in the Taliban are on the run, but what you have done today may help to reverse that defeat."

Without saying goodbye, the man cut the connection.

Shafiq looked at the phone and went back to the seat he had previously occupied. He put a quarter in the television set attached to the seat and watched news reports of the crash on CNN. He had done his work well and tomorrow, Allah willing, he would be home.

———— ◉ ————

John Williams stood in awe of everything that was going on at the Beachcomber office. The young reporter had been working for the paper for only four months when the towers came down. It was a tough time, covering funerals, speaking with relatives of the 75 local people who had died in that attack. Now, he was too busy to think of anything but covering the plane crash.

Four months ago he had graduated from Queens College. Today, he was actively working an international story.

He thought that he would probably spend a few years with the Beachcomber before moving on to a daily paper, or perhaps a television job. He thought that he would be covering community meetings and local politicians, but today he was acting as an informant for the world's media giants.

John was on the phone with the Boston Globe. That paper wanted to do an in-depth sidebar on local people who had lost a relative in the World Trade Center and now had been impacted by the plane crash.

The Globe reporter wanted names and telephone numbers, something that Williams did not want to supply.

"I'm not sure that I can give you that information without asking the families first," Williams said, for the third time. He was not getting through to the Globe reporter, who obviously had an assignment to get the story and a deadline that was coming closer with each minute.

"Why not? Don't you cooperate with out of town papers," the reporter asked.

Williams was exasperated. He wanted to get off the phone.

"Sure we do," he answered. "If the request is reasonable. We're a local, community paper. We don't dump on our readers and we don't intrude on their lives or their grief to get a story."

He slammed down the phone.

Williams was a little miffed that he had been told to stay at the office and handle whatever came in rather than rushing to the scene with his Staller. He understood the need for one person on the two-person staff to stay put, but he would have loved to cover his first massive local story on the scene.

Staller came up behind him.

"Way to go, John," Staller said. "That's the way to handle those pushy out of towner's. Save your help and sources for the locals."

John smiled. He and Staller got along well though their outlook on life and their take on lots of issues was very different. John was the first African American to work full time for the paper, and he often believed he carried an extra burden because of that fact. His end of the peninsula, the eastern end, had never been well served by the paper, he believed and he was going to change that. Now, the biggest story in years comes along and it's a west end story all the way.

"John, grab your camera and go over to Peninsula Hospital. Find out how many people they've admitted and take some pictures," Staller said.

Glad to finally get out of the office, Williams took his camera bag and left for the nearby medical facility. Staller yelled to him as he walked out the door.

"I just heard on the scanner that the cops are closing the bridges off the peninsula. They think the crash might be an act of terrorism. Get some shots of the cops blocking off the approaches to the Cross Bay Bridge while you're out. We'll do a page on how the crash affected the other people on the peninsula."

Williams waved and left the office.

The phone rang again.

"Ron, Line 2," the receptionist said over the intercom.

"Ron Staller," he said, as he punched the button for line 2.

"Listen carefully," the voice said. "I am an Arab Christian who works at the airport. I was ordered by Yasar Arafat to sabotage the plane so that it would fall on Belle Harbor. There are many Jews living there," the voice said.

"Could I have your name, sir," Staller asked. "I'm sure that the FBI would be interested in your story."

The contact was broken with a loud click.

Staller smiled. "They were surely going to come out of the woodwork on this one," he thought to himself.

While most of the calls would be from kooks, he thought, there might be some truth in one or two. He was glad he had instituted a pen register log on the Beachcomber's phones. Every call was logged by date, time and caller's telephone number. Perhaps he would check when he had some time and see who had made the calls. Right now, however, that was not a priority.

"Line one, Ron," the voice on the intercom said with a tired demeanor. He hit the button.

"I can't give you my name, and I can't call the cops for my own personal reasons, but I saw a couple of guys on a boat out on the bay and they fired a missile from a boat off the diner. I watched it streak into the sky and explode near the plane," the male voice said. "Check out the damage to the plane, it has to show the explosion. I know what I'm talking about." Before Ron could answer, the line clicked off.

"Ron, there's somebody up front to see you," came the disembodied voice over the intercom, disturbing his thoughts about his last caller, probably another crank, but his story seemed possible. His was a community paper, and local people were always coming to the front office with story tips, notes about birthdays and pictures of their pets.

Staller went to the front of the office. A man was standing there.

"I saw the plane get hit," he said quickly, as if he wanted to get his story out before it went away. "I saw the missile chase it down Rockaway Beach Boulevard. It was a Navy jet that shot it down. I'll bet the plane was heading for the Empire State Building and the President ordered that the Navy shoot it down. I saw the missile, plain as day."

Staller took his name and telephone number and thanked him for his help. The man left, satisfied that his story would be told.

He went back to handle several more telephone calls from media outlets all over the world.

One of those was from WTOP in Washington, D.C. The producer of their nightly news show asked if Ken would meet the station's on-air reporter for a quick interview at 7:30 p.m. at Beach 130 and Cronston Avenue, only a block for the crash scene.

Staller agreed. He asked the producer how he would identify the reporter.

"Tammy Jones is blonde, very pretty, and thin and she'll be wearing jeans and a short, black leather jacket. She'll be wearing station press credentials and she'll expect you.

At the appointed time, Staller walked from his parked car to the corner or Beach 130 and Cronston. On each corner, there was a television truck and crew. On each corner, there was a blonde, very pretty female reporter wearing jeans and a short leather jacket each wearing press credentials around their neck. Confused, he stood in the middle of the street, trying to figure out what he was going to do next.

Three of the reporters were doing interviews with local residents, firefighters or local officials. The fourth walked up to Staller.

"Looking for somebody," she asked?

"I'm supposed to be interviewed by the reporter from WTOP."

"Who are you?"

"Ron Staller, the editor of the local paper, the Beachcomber."

"My name is Sheila Puljos," the woman said. "I'm a reporter for WBBM in Boston. Everybody seems to be busy now. Would you do a quick standup with me?"

"Sure, why not," Staller answered.

The WBBM producer placed Staller so that his back was to the accident scene. Puljos stood to his side, introduced him, and shoved the mike at his face.

"And, Mr. Staller, where were you when the plane came down? Describe what you saw at the crash scene when you first got there."

Staller answered. The interview took about four minutes before it was wrapped up.

Another of the blonde women approached Staller.

She introduced herself and asked if he were ready to do the interview. It was a repeat of the last interview. Staller was getting into the flow, anticipating the questions and adding flourishes to his answers. This was getting interesting, maybe even fun.

Reaza Mahobir was lost and she couldn't believe that she was still in her home borough of Queens. A Newsday reporter who had been recently hired to cover the growing immigrant communities in central and northern Queens, she was way off her beat, but when the managing editor called and told her to get to Rockaway and cover the plane crash, she jumped in her car and drove south, knowing vaguely that Rockaway was south of JFK Airport, between Jamaica Bay and the ocean. She just didn't know which roads would get her there.

Reaza adjusted her headscarf and looked around. They had told her on her cell phone to take the Van Wyck Expressway to the Belt Parkway west to Cross Bay Boulevard, but construction crews were working on the new Air train tracks high above the expressway and she had been forced off onto unfamiliar side streets. The green street signs she was looking at read "Liberty Avenue" and "120th Street, but they might as well have said "Calcutta" as far as Reaza was concerned.

The car in front of her began moving and she followed it, looking for a street name that sounded familiar. She saw none.

"How could I be so stupid not to bring a map," she said aloud. She made a mental note to pick up a book of New York City maps the next chance she got.

The head covering and lose garments that Reaza wore could not really cover the fact that she was a beautiful and sensuous women. The fact that she was Muslim and was extremely good-looking had helped her get the job with Newsday, a paper that was actively courting the new immigrants communities, many of them Middle Eastern and Asian, springing up all over the borough. Her talent and her ability to find a story in every situation helped her keep it.

Now, however, she was out of her depth, assigned to cover the crash of flight 587 in Rockaway, to find women who had been affected both by the attack on the World Trade Center and by this latest tragedy.

She laughed to herself, "How can I get the story if I can't even find Rockaway?"

Reaza stopped the car next to a tuxedo rental firm that had closed for the day. She took out her computer and dialed up the internet on her cell phone, a phone that included a modem hookup to her computer.

When the internet appeared, she quickly typed in "Mapquest," a mapping website that would give her step by step directions. She typed in the cross streets where the car stood and then, checking her notebook, "Belle Harbor, 11694." It took only a minute for the site to generate a map that showed Reaza that she was only few blocks from Cross Bay Boulevard. She was relieved. She was not so far off track.

On a whim, she typed "Rockaway newspaper" into the search engine. The hard drive chugged for a moment and then the names and address for the Beachcomber appeared. She wrote the paper's phone number in her notebook, logged off the internet and turned off her computer.

Then she dialed the paper's number on her cell phone.

"If anybody can help me get this story, it's going to be the local paper," she thought as she put the car in gear and headed for Belle Harbor.

———————◦«(◦)»◦———————

Tommy Lewis sat in his Wavecrest Gardens apartment on Seagirt Boulevard at the eastern end of Rockaway, not far from the Nassau County border, watching the news about the crash of flight 587 on his television set. He had stashed the piece of plane he had taken from the crash scene in the back of the ambulance garage in nearby Inwood right over the county line in Nassau County. Nobody would look for it there, he figured, and if anybody found it, they probably would not know what it was in any case.

He was sure that he could make some money on the aircraft part. If the television reporter was right, this was the second worst aircraft accident in American history.

The debris should be worth something.

He walked to his small kitchen, looking for a beer. As he did, he glanced over at his computer. The thought came to him.

"I'll sell it on E-bay," he said aloud. "Damn, why didn't I think of that earlier?"

He went over and booted up his computer, impatiently watching it go through the start-up procedure. When his desktop came up, he double-clicked on the AOL icon. Soon, he was looking at the AOL welcome screen.

"You have mail," the familiar computerized voice said.

He checked his mail. Some SPAM, some jokes forwarded to him by friends and acquaintances. Nothing that he wanted to spend any time on.

He clicked on "favorites" and then on "E-bay."

He had sold many items on the auction site, and he quickly entered his latest item for sale. He had learned from experience that you could sell anything on E-bay. There were some even selling memorabilia from the World Trade Center attack for hundreds of dollars. He would cash in with this piece of flight 587.

He got to the "Sell" screen and typed in his password.

"A piece of Aircraft Wreckage from a recent aircraft crash," he entered. Then, he typed in a description of the item, "a fairly large piece of wreckage from American Airlines Flight 587, which crashed in Rockaway on November 12. Guaranteed to be the real thing, a rare collector's item for aviation buffs. "

"That should set the hook," he thought to himself. He would ask for $75 as his starting price. "Let the suckers bid it up," he said aloud with a chuckle. "Let's see how high they will go."

—————————— ((O)) ——————————

"Ron, Line three," the receptionist cried out, probably for the hundredth time that afternoon. Staller was almost tired of taking calls from all over the world, but he decided that he had to get through this and still put out the paper on Thursday. It was going to be a tough week all around.

He picked up the phone and hit the "three" button.

"Staller," he said.

"This is Reaza Mahobir, a reporter for Newsday," the soothing voice at the other end said quietly. "I'm on my way to Rockaway to do a sidebar on the crash and thought that you might be able to help me. Could I take about ten minutes of your time sometime in the near future?"

Staller was intrigued with the voice. The speaker had a lilt and a slight accent that was pleasing to the ear.

"Sure," Staller answered. "Where are you now?"

"I'm not sure," Reaza said with a laugh. "I've already been lost three or four times today trying to find Rockaway. Right now I'm going south on Cross Bay Boulevard, just passing a place called Broad Channel. Am I close?"

"Just about five minutes away, if the police let you go across the Cross Bay Bridge. I hear they have it closed, but your press credentials should get you through."

"Why is the bridge closed? Did the plane hit it?

"No, but somebody is concerned that the crash was part of a terrorist attack, so they've closed all the bridges again, just like they did after 9-11."

Staller gave her directions from the bridge, which she now saw was in front of her and was, indeed, closed by police cars.

She thanked Staller and pushed the "end" button to close the call and took out her press credentials. In minutes, she was across the bridge and heading for the Beachcomber office.

Ron was on the phone with BBC-Australia when the receptionist told him that he had a visitor.

He quickly ended the call and walked up to the front counter, hoping that it was the Newsday reporter that had called. He was anxious to see the woman that went with the delightful voice. The woman that he saw standing in front of the receptionist matched his expectations. She was slim and beautiful, despite the headscarf and loose fitting clothing that she wore.

He introduced himself and escorted her into the small newsroom.

"Thanks for making time for me on such a busy day. I know what it must be like," Reaza said.

He told Carol to put a hold on all of his calls for a few minutes.

"I needed a break from the phone," he said, a little too quickly. "What can I do for you?"

"I want to interview some women who lost somebody on September 11 and were also impacted by today's accident. Do you know anybody who would fit that bill? It's for a sidebar to go with the main accident story."

Staller thought for a moment.

"It's a little early to know that," he answered. He looked above his head where the front pages of all the papers since September hung in a line. He pointed to the September 29 issue. Down the side of the page was a list of 73 local residents who had died in the World Trade Center a month before.

"There's the list. The plane came down right down the street from Cliff Mapes and his wife. I saw him fighting the fire in the gas station today."

"Is he a firefighter?"

"No, his brother was, but his brother was lost when the Trade Center came down. His wife might make a good interview for you. She's a teacher in the public school two blocks from where the plane came down."

"Sounds perfect. Can you put me in touch with her?"

Ron pulled out his PDA and called up the name he was looking for. He gave the number to Reaza and indicated that she could use the phone on his desk.

Just then, there was a call over the intercom.

"Ron, your son is here to see you."

"Send him back," Ron yelled.

Ken Staller, still in uniform, walked into the newsroom area.

"I came up to make sure you were OK," Ken said without preamble.

"I'm fine, why are you worried about me? I was more worried about you. I went to your house, but you were gone."

"Knowing you, I figured you were standing under the plane when it came down," Ken joked.

Ron realized that his son was speaking to him, but he was staring at Reaza.

He made introductions.

Reaza and Ken gingerly shook hands.

"Were you at the scene, Sergeant Staller," she asked.

"I got there late, but I was there until just now," he answered.

"What can you tell me," she asked. In the best traditions of journalism, she was not going to miss a chance to interview a cop who might know something she did not already know.

"Not much," he answered. "I know that there is going to be a news conference at St. Francis Church in about an hour. The mayor and the police commissioner will be there. Maybe the governor, if they can get his copter in."

"Not my beat," she answered. "Somebody else will cover that. I am going to call this lead your dad gave me for my sidebar and see if I can interview her tonight."

Reaza picked up the phone, dialed nine and then the number that Staller had given her.

The Stallers wandered away to give her a little privacy.

"How bad is it," Ron asked his son.

"We were lucky. More like a miracle. Only five reported dead on the ground. Everybody on the plane. It will take a couple of days to get all the bodies out of there."

Reaza hung up the phone and walked towards the two men.

"She'll talk to me now. If you can give me directions, that's where I'm headed. She checked her notes. She lives on Beach 129 between Rockaway Beach Boulevard and Newport Avenue.

"I live right up the block from there," Ken said. "I'm heading back to the command post at the church. Why don't you follow me, and I'll get you through the roadblocks. There is one at Beach 116 and the Boulevard that only allows local residents into area."

Reaza smiled.

"Thanks," she said. "That would be great."

Ken said goodbye to his father and walked out with Reaza.

Ron turned back to the phones, which were once again ringing off the hook.

V

R on Staller was startled when the radio alarm went off at 5:30 a.m. It had been a tough night, with interviews into the late hours and then a call from BBC Australia at 2:30 a.m. The Aussies, who had somehow tracked down his home number, wondered if he would he be available to give a live interview for their morning show? Of course, he would. His late-night actions were taking a toll on him, however. At 62, he wasn't getting any younger.

He quickly plugged in the Mr. Coffee and took a shower while it brewed. He had to be at Beach 130th Street and Rockaway Beach Boulevard by 6:15 a.m. The show's producer told him that he would be doing a live interview with Lauer, one of the co-hosts of the "Today" show at 7:30, but he was told that he had to be ready for sound checks and other arcane events by 6:45.

"Yesterday at this time, I was just another retired teacher trying to find a second career that was a lot more fun than the first," he thought. "Today, thanks to a random act like a plane crashing on my beat, I'm going to be on national television."

Omar, who had been a Saudi Arabian intelligence officer long enough to know that attacks never went exactly as planned, had mixed feelings about the day just past. He had been up most of the night, checking out his handiwork on CNN, as well as waiting for the latest news from Afghanistan. He hoped that the updated reports would tell of a Taliban counterattack. The attack on the airliner had gone far better than he had expected. The plan was to bring down the airliner shortly after takeoff, with the off-chance that it would crash into a populated area, but there was always more of a chance that it would crash into either Jamaica Bay or the Atlantic Ocean. It was a plus, he thought, that it came down on land, even though it only killed five locals. He could not remember the name of the community where it came down. He was even happier that nobody, at least to his knowledge, had connected the crash with a missile attack. In fact, George Pataki, the governor of New York State, had quickly announced that the crash was an accident and not an act of terrorism.

"Timing is everything," he thought. "Osama and my Saudi bosses will be happy with me, with the operation."

On the other hand, neither he nor Osama, nor even the Saudi king would be happy about the news from Kabul, the fall of the capital city of Afghanistan earlier that day. It was a definite setback, one that would not easily be offset by the success of taking down a large airliner. Somehow, he did not like the fact that one event deflated the importance of the other. He was hoping for special recognition from the Sheik himself for his JFK operations, but now everyone was focused on Afghanistan.

Omar looked out of the window of his Ozone Park apartment. There were many Muslim immigrants living in the area, a number of mosques to attend. He fit in just fine with his surroundings. Hearing the familiar sounds of aircraft engines, he looked up. An American Airlines 747 was about 120 feet above his head, inbound to JFK. He was glad to see the planes flying again. It would mean that Tafiq and Sayed would soon be heading home. The longer they stayed in New York, the greater their exposure.

He walked to his computer and booted it up. He would search the web for stories about the crash of flight 587, he would see if anybody had evidence that it was indeed a terrorist act, any reports of a missile or smoke rising from the bay. Not that anybody would buy it. He thought of TWA Flight 800, which had been brought down over Long Island. Hundreds of people, some with pictures and even videos, had reported a missile trail coming out of the water before the plane exploded. The government had ignored all of their stories and it would do the same for Flight 587 if anybody saw the missile. He was not sure why the American government would want to cover up an attack, but it was clear that it was not ready to admit that it was vulnerable. Perhaps the aircraft industry wanted the public to believe that their planes were safe from attack. Perhaps American leaders were just incompetent. It did not matter much either way to Omar. Either way, his team was in the clear.

After getting the news, he thought, he would go onto E-bay and buy some more American treasures to take home to Afghanistan. In his three short years in America, he had become an E-bay junkie. In fact, there were many delights in America that he would miss when he was ordered back to either Saudi Arabia or Afghanistan.

⸻ ⸺◍⸻ ⸻

Bobby Sallow came out of the apartment early to get the daily paper. After yesterday's events, he quickly looked around to see if anybody was watching him. He knew that he was paranoid, that nobody was looking for him any longer. He was far from his old life, from his wife, who lived in the Bronx. He had seen his name on the list of the World Trade Center Dead. He had read of the memorial service that his wife was planning in his memory. He snickered when she was interviewed by Channel Five News and proclaimed her undying love for him. She was probably glad to get rid of him and was more interested in looking for a large payday. He was dead, at least, officially. There were so many television people around after the crash, however, and the last thing he wanted was to get his face on television. Somebody who knew him in his previous life might recognize him and then his bitchy wife would find him. It was worth all the money she was going to get for him to be rid of her, to have a chance for a real life with Toni.

Thinking about his wife brought back the events a month ago. After the Navy, he had gone to work for Cantor Fitzgerald as a bond salesman. At least, until September 11, he thought with a smile.

"I'm not going to miss my wife and I'm not going to miss that job one bit either," he thought to himself.

He was late to work at his One World Trade Center office on the morning of September 11 because he had stopped in a nearby store to buy a birthday present for Toni. When he came out of the store, the first building, his building, was on fire. He turned around, grabbed the A Train and headed for Rockaway. It was only when the train cleared the tunnel at Rockaway Boulevard and moved out over Jamaica Bay that he started to think of the future. It was then that he started to develop the plan that he was following with Toni.

"They'll never find all the bodies," he told her. "They'll think that I was at my desk, that I'm dead. I'm free. I never have to go back to my wife, to my job. To the world, I'm already dead."

The train pulled into the Beach 116th Street Station and Bobby stopped for a coffee at the Last Stop restaurant. Everybody was talking about the attack. People were lined up across Beach Channel Drive, at the seawall on Jamaica Bay, watching the smoke come from Manhattan across the bay.

"How am I going to explain all of this to Toni," he wondered. "Especially on her birthday."

That was more than two months ago. He and Toni had spent that night watching television, talking about their future. She was actually happy, if a little worried about how it would play out. The past two months had proven that his plan would work perfectly.

Sallow, assured that there were no television cameras in the area, walked around to the side of the house, hoping to see the newspaper propped up on a tree.

He was disappointed that it was not there, when he heard a thump against the door of the apartment house. He went to get the paper and quickly went to Toni's apartment. He could not wait to see the paper, to find out if somebody else had also seen what he saw.

Toni and Bobby had walked to the local steak house the night before. Everybody was talking about the crash. Several people repeated stories that they had heard during the day, stories that said that many people had seen fire and smoke on the fuselage of the plane before it crashed, but nobody had heard that a missile had brought down the plan.

Bobby opened the paper and looked at the front page. There was a large picture of the crash scene taken by somebody from the local paper, The Beachcomber. All the stories talked about the fact that the crash was probably an accident.

"How could that be," he asked himself. "Didn't anybody else see the missile?"

"Damn it," he thought to himself. "No news stories about the missile that I saw hit the plane. What are the papers waiting for?"

A thought struck him. "Maybe they know," he said aloud to himself. "Maybe they know and they're covering it up."

In any case, there was nothing he could do, nobody he could speak with. He was beginning to think that being dead was not such a hot idea after all.

―――――――⟨⟨●⟩⟩―――――――

The interview with Matt Lauer had gone well. There was no way it could have been otherwise. A researcher for the show had pumped him for good stories about the crash, about the community. Those stories were then translated into questions for Lauer to ask him.

The eight minute interview seemed like twenty, however, and Staller was sweating when he finished despite the chill in the air and the wind coming off the ocean.

As an example of the resiliency of local residents, he had told the story of a woman whose house had been wiped out by the plane. She had been at work at a local doctor's office at the time of the crash, but all of her belongings, including her clothing had been destroyed by the ensuing fire. Invited to a wedding that weekend, she asked the bride if she could come in what she was wearing – she had no other clothing and all of her credit cards and cash had been in the house. The story had come to Staller through the bride, who was the daughter of an old school colleague.

Staller did not know it at the time, but his office was already getting calls from major department stores offering the woman a new free dress, shoes and accessories to wear to the wedding.

He headed back for the office, knowing that it was Tuesday and his team had done little to get ready for the paper's Thursday deadline because of all of the excitement the day previously.

He would have to fudge it a bit. Several pages of pictures, some eyewitness stories, a report from the NTSB, his eyewitness account of the aftermath, a list of the dead. In any case, it was going to be a long couple of days between now and Thursday evening, when the paper was put to bed and sent to the printing facility in Long Island City.

———◦《◉》◦———

Omar was on the Internet, trolling his favorite sites. He had finished reporting to his sources in the Middle East using imbedded text inside jpg photos. The return report from the organization's leadership revealed that they were proud of his efforts on behalf of the cause. He had watched his television set most of the night, watching what he and the others had done.

The first reports from the NTSB and other government sources were that the crash was an accident, that he pilot had somehow torn the tail off the aircraft by over controlling the rudder.

"Stupid people," he thought to himself. "They don't even understand that they are under attack."

He logged onto E-Bay and checked his "My E-Bay" page to see how his bids were doing. Several were up that day and he wanted to check them carefully. It was nice to have an unlimited amount of American dollars to pay with.

He typed "Flight 587" into the search engine, figuring that he might find a flight schedule or a ticket stub from a previous flight of a similar aircraft.

What he saw, however, made him sit up and concentrate on the screen.

Somebody with the screen name of "busdriver" was selling a piece of the wreckage. That was not good. The wreckage was the operation's Trojan horse. Had the plane fallen into the ocean or the bay, the wreckage would not be a problem. With the plane parts scattered all over Rockaway, however, he realized somebody might determine just what brought the plane down, although he doubted it, but there was always a chance of something going wrong.

Now, this "busdriver" was selling a piece on the web.

He moved through the screens until he saw the seller's E-mail address.

"Good," he thought, "He's on AOL."

He quickly logged off E-Bay and went to AOL. Within minutes, using Google, the person's name, his AOL profile and some information from a few other more specialized sites he had wisely purchased when he first came to America, he had the seller's name and address.

He logged off. He needed a plan – one that would get him that piece of wreckage before it could be closely scrutinized. So far, he thought, nobody had identified the crash as an attack, and he wanted to keep it that way.

VI

Ron Staller was already at this desk at The Beachcomber, writing the lead story for that week's paper. Because the paper was a weekly and came out on Friday morning, he had to localize the story to his readership, because everybody who lived in his coverage area would already know the basic facts about the crash long before the paper came out on Friday, November 17, the next publication date.

He would do some interviews that morning with those who claimed that they saw the plane on fire while it was still in the air. He would write an editorial that he planned to call "Coming Out Of The Woodwork," about all of the strange calls the paper had received and all of the theories of why the plane crashed. He would write his weekly column about the problems that came with the world's focus on his little community. He had lots to do.

Although it was still about an hour before most of the newspaper's staff and artists came to work, Ron heard the door to the small newsroom open and saw John Williams walk in.

"Good morning, you're early today," Ron said in way of greeting.

"Lot's to do," William answered in his normal taciturn manner. "How are we going to play this?"

"We had some calls from folks who say that they saw the plane explode in the air, or at least that they saw fire on the fuselage prior to the crash. Most of them sound credible," Ron answered. "I want to interview some of them this morning, if I can reach them. I want you to work with the artists on a four-page spread of pictures. There are lots of prints that we scanned in yesterday from Steve and Dennis and some other people who were at the site. Mine are there too, and the digital pictures we have are in a folder called '587 Pix.'"

The phone rang.

Because none of the front-end staff was in as yet, Staller answered the call himself.

"The Beachcomber, Ron Staller, can I help you?"

"Hey, Ron, it's Tony Weiner," the familiar voice said. Weiner was the local Congressman, a favorite of his who visited the newspaper office whenever he was in the area. "I've got a statement for you if you're ready and you have room this week."

Staller picked up a pad and pencil.

"Shoot. Always have room for you."

"I sent a letter to the FAA calling on all flights out of Kennedy to fly the "Bridge Route" out over the bay and the Marine Parkway Bridge and then back over the ocean to their waypoint," He said. "Planes should not cut over the peninsula. There is no good reason why an airport built on the water should not use water routing when it available."

"We're going to propose penalties for any airline that diverts its planes over the peninsula," he added. He gave Staller a quick quote to use with the story and his condolences to the families who died in the crash, both in Rockaway and on the plane.

"That's it. Can you get it in?"

"Sure. Thanks and I'll call if I need anything else," Staller said, breaking the connection.

The phone rang again, and Staller answered it, thinking that he should call his front end people in early for the next week or so. Have to pay them extra for the extended day, but it would be worth it.

"Beachcomber, Staller," he said.

"What's up," a familiar voice asked.

It was his son, Ken.

"Getting an early start on a long day."

"Yeah, I know. Have to be over at the command post in a couple of minutes and thought you'd like to know that I just got the word that the Governor is going to be here today." He'll be at the diner.at about 11:30. Copter's going to drop him at the Beach Channel High School field. I have to get an escort ready."

"Thanks for the head's up. I'll send John to cover it. Will they have a press availability?"

"When did you ever know a politician that did not let the press have access for their sound bites and pictures," his son joked.

"We're going to set up some press raisers across from the diner on the bay," his son added. "Some pool photographers and network types will be allowed into the diner to get him while he mixes with the locals. I'm sure as a local you can get inside."

"Talk to Tammy," he added, referring to the director of the local chamber of commerce. "She's setting it up."

"Thanks," Ron said. "I'll do that right now. Have a good tour. Maybe I'll see you at the command post. It's still at St. Francis?"

"Yeah," his son responded. "See you later."

The connection was broken, and immediately, the phone rang again.

"The Beachcomber, Ron Staller," he answered. "Can I help you?"

"Hi, Ron, this is Reaza Mahobir from Newsday. How are you to-day," the soft, melodious voice answered.

"On deadline, as usual," Ron answered with a laugh, knowing that another newspaper person would know what that meant.

"I won't keep you but a moment. I wanted to thank you for Tuesday and for pointing me to your son. He was a big help. I am going to be out in Rockaway today for the governor's visit. I thought I would stop in and touch base with the locals. Would that be OK?"

"Sure, I have one of my reporters covering the governor," he said, not adding that it was his only reporter. "I'll be here doing phone interviews and writing most of the day."

"Will your son be around?"

"I just spoke with him. He's planning on being with the governor and then at the command post."

"Maybe I'll bump into him somewhere along the way. Thanks again, Ron, see you later."

Staller hung up, debating with himself as to whether he should share some of his local contacts with Reaza. He would have to see how it worked out.

He checked the phone list he had retrieved from his caller identification system he began to keep since Tuesday and noted some numbers he had to call. The first call was to be the number of the person who called saying he had seen a missile bring down 587.

He called the number and got no response, not even an answering machine, which he thought was kind of strange. He made a mental note to call back that night, when somebody would probably be home.

⸻))(() ((⸻

Staller turned back to the production of that week's Beachcomber.

He had to shuffle computer stations in the small newsroom, which hosted five computers, with a sixth in the rear of the building. Reporters from The Washington Post, the Boston Globe, the Denver Post and the Philadelphia Bulletin had been in and out of the office, using his phones and his computers as their own – with his permission, of course. Some of them were due in later this morning. He would be glad when things quieted down, but he had to admit all the hustle was exciting and he enjoyed speaking with the reporters from all over the nation, sharing his Rockaway expertise.

He spent some time working with his staff, putting together three pages of photos and meeting with the art director to come up with just the right front page photo. It was decided that the cover would include a large color photo, something unusual for the Beachcomber. It was the first time that the paper had used color on the front page, and he hoped it would not be the last, convincing himself that it worth the extra cost for such a major story.

One of the photos in the mix was the shot he had taken in the gas station of the engines in the bay, but his team decided on a blazing fire shot instead, convinced that the bright red color would draw people to the newsstand.

He wrote the editorial about the crazies who had been calling with conspiracy theories about the crash and added a small second editorial that he called "Closing the Barn Door," using Tony Weiner's proposal that planes be restricted from flying over the peninsula.

He called the Peninsula Hospital Center on Beach 51 Street and spoke with its public outreach director. None of the people who were on the plane had been treated, of course. There were 46 patients treated as a result of the crash, however, most of them cops and firefighters who suffered smoke inhalation fighting the fires and looking for survivors among the homes at the crash site. Only four of them had to be admitted and one had suffered a heart attack and was transferred to a Nassau County hospital that specialized in cardiac emergencies.

The local chamber of commerce had called to announce that there was going to be a public contest to design a memorial to those who died in 9/11 as well as in the crash of Flight 587.

And, there were obituaries to write for the five locals who had died in the fire.

Staller set up a shaded box on the front page with the names of the five locals, honoring them in death. He had lots of work to do before the Thursday deadline.

He called American Airlines public relations probably for the fifth time, looking for a list of the crew and passengers who died on the plane. He wanted to honor them as well, but was told that the passenger list was not yet available for publication because some of the next of kin could not be found for the mandatory notifications to be made. He was told to call back in a few hours. By then, it would be too late to publish the list this week. He noticed that the New York Times had a list and wondered if he should just copy that, counting on that paper to have the correct names. He logged off and got ready to go to work, deciding that he would use the Time list and hope for the best. Obviously, while the Times was a priority for the airlines, the Beachcomber was not.

————))(((•))((————

Omar stood in the cold outside of the Wavecrest Gardens building on Crest Road, where Lewis lived. Parked in a space nearby was the car that Lewis would hopefully use to get to work. He checked the license plate one more time. It was the right plate. He had run it off the Motor Vehicle Department's computers just hours ago. He loved American technology. It made everything so much easier.

He had no picture of Lewis, but he assumed that whoever got into the car would be the man who perhaps held, without knowing it, a key piece in the Flight 587 mystery.

He would not live to sell it, nor would he live to talk about it.

First, however, Omar would have to find out just where that wreckage was located. He would do that by following Lewis until he found it.

————))(((•))((————

New York State Governor George Pataki had just finished brunch in the Sunset Diner. Pataki, sitting at the counter across the bay from JFK Airport, had hosted a meeting of local residents, activists journalists and politicians. His copter had dropped him at the Beach Channel High School athletic field, just 15 blocks from the diner, not far from the spot where the tail of flight 587 was pulled from the bay.

The brunch had given Pataki a chance to be seen in the accident zone talking with locals, insuring them that the crash was a tragic accident and that the NTSB had taken the lead in the investigation of the causes of the crash.

"There is no evidence of terrorism in the tragic crash here in Rockaway," Pataki said to the bank of television cameras at the rear of the diner and to the print journalists elbowing each other for space to write their notes and take their pictures. "The NTSB has assured me just this morning, before I came to Rockaway, that the twisted metal left at the crash scene shows no indication of explosion nor of fire."

Reaza, who had been assigned to cover the governor's appearance – a good sign, she decided -- spoke up loudly with a question.

"A number of eyewitnesses here in Rockaway have told reporters that they saw fire on the fuselage and explosions prior to the crash. How can you account for those reports?"

"Well, the NTSB has taken over the lead in the investigation rather than the FBI because they are convinced that the crash had no terrorist ties, no criminal act," Pataki answered. "Eyewitnesses are usually unreliable in this type of accident, because they factor in what they saw in movies and television shows that depicted accidents. Experts tell me that they really believe what they think they saw, but they did not actually see what they believed and reported they did."

"A follow-up, if I might," Reaza said quickly. "Many of the eyewitnesses are police officers and firefighters with 20 or more years on the job. Can't these professionals be expected to be reliable witnesses, even to the most horrendous accident?"

"The twisted metal tells the story," the governor said with finality "There is nothing more to say."

"Now," the governor added, "If you will excuse me, I have to get back to work. Thank you all for inviting me."

With his protective detail trailing in his wake, Pataki left the diner, shaking hands as he went.

"You didn't really expect him to answer that question, did you," a voice said from behind Reaza.

She turned and saw Sergeant Staller standing there, looking at her.

"Ken," she said, genuinely glad to see him. "It's good to see you again."

"The powers-that-be have decided that this was an accident, and nothing anybody can tell them will make any difference," Staller said. "You might as well save your breath."

"I don't see your dad here," she said, changing the subject.

"His reporter is here shooting pictures. I guess he's back at the office, putting out the paper."

"How is your women's story going," he asked.

"Finished. It seems that my editors figured that if I'm already here, I should cover some of the hard news stuff as well."

"Sounds good. Do you enjoy that more than the features?"

"Of course. I've wanted to get on the metro desk for a long time. Perhaps this will do it for me."

"What time do you finish covering the story today," Staller asked, blushing.

"Why?"

"I thought we could have dinner together later, if you are free," he answered.

Reaza thought for a moment.

"I'll be finished here about four and then I have to send in my story for tomorrow's Queens Edition, she said. "As much as I would like to have dinner with you tonight, the time is off, just too tight. I'd like to take a raincheck. How about Friday night.

He suggested a local restaurant and she tentatively agreed, making it clear that her schedule was always dictated by unfolding events, as his was as well.

"See you then," Reaza said, closing her notebook and walking out the door.

Staller walked out of the diner and watched Reaza get into her car and drive away. He looked forward to the evening to come. Reaza was a very beautiful and interesting woman, he thought.

He spotted two of the detectives from the 100 Precinct Squad standing nearby the bay wall, across the street from the diner. He crossed Beach Channel Drive and walked up to them.

Staller had known Billy Droesch for many years. He was a second grade detective whose family owned a Bar, "The Blarney Castle" on

Beach 116th Street. His partner, Richie Cohen, was relatively new to the precinct, having come from the 101 Squad at the other end of the peninsula only a few months before.

Staller had graduated from the academy with Droesch, but had not worked with him for some time. He knew that Droesch and Cohen had "caught" the crash, which meant that it was their case. He also knew, however, that the FBI and the NTSB has declared the crash an accident and there was no longer an active criminal investigation going despite the 265 deaths.

Droesch and Cohen, however, would continue to work the accident as a crime until they were satisfied that it was not. Or, until their bosses told them to put it on the back burner.

"How are you doing, Billy," Staller asked as he walked up to the two detectives.

"Ken, how is the chief treating you," Droesch asked with a smile.

"Getting along," he answered. "You got anything at all on the crash?"

"Nothing yet. Lots of statements to go through. About fifty people say they saw the plane in the air and that it was on fire before it hit the ground. Some say they saw explosions. Others say that the saw explosions and fire. There's shit from the plane scattered from 108 Street to Gateway. Hard to figure out."

"Are you still working it?'

"What do you think? Could be 265 homicides, although it doesn't look like Fart, Barf and Itch will ever admit it."

Staller laughed to himself at the typical NYPD name for the FBI. He had used it many times himself and that was only the mildest of the names for the federal crime fighting agency that could be heard at police headquarters at One Police Plaza, better known as 1PP or the Puzzle Palace.

Staller wanted to get back to the command post and finish the day. In the back of his mine, however, was the thought that something was wrong with the governor's assertion that the crash was definitely an accident. That didn't jibe with what Droesch had told him about the eyewitnesses.

"Let me know if you get anything I should know about," Staller said.

"You got it," Droesch answered. See ya."

Staller went back to the command post at St. Francis de Sales Church. Volunteers were still serving food and drinks to rescue workers and investigators. Lots of police officers, NTSB investigators and firefighters could be seen mingling with the press.

VII

2200 HOURS
14 NOVEMBER, 2001

O mar waited for Tommy Lewis to leave his apartment
house. He had to follow him until he found out where the
piece of wreckage was located. It was important that the
wreckage that Lewis found not be turned over to investigators.
The only flaw in the destruction of flight 587 was that it fell onto
Rockaway rather than in either Jamaica Bay or the Atlantic Ocean.
Had the wreckage gone down into water, it probably would not
have been recovered. Now, however, he was surprised that investigators continued to say that the crash was an accident. He
knew that some of the debris from the plane would show explosive residue.

"Surely, by now they can see where the missile fragments hit
the fuselage," he thought.

He couldn't take any chances, however. He had to have the piece
of the plane that Lewis was trying to sell on E-bay. While he knew
rationally that the government had the rest of the debris, which un-
doubtedly showed missile damage, it was just as clear that there was
a movement at high levels to cover up that fact. He just wanted to
make sure that nobody but the government had the proof of the missile because he did not want some whistle-blower to go to the papers
or CNN with the evidence.

A movement at the apartment house door caught Omar's eye. ..A
man was coming out of the back door of the large apartment building
and walking towards Lewis' car.

He sat lower in his seat. The man passed him and started Lewis' car. This had to be him. As he drove away, Omar followed.

The two cars came out of Crest Road and made a right turn on Seagirt Boulevard heading east, towards Nassau County on Long Island. It was not easy for Omar to follow Lewis without being seen, because there were few cars on the six-lane road that time of night. The cars passed a large four-building complex on the right and then bypassed signs that foretold a turnoff for the Atlantic Beach Bridge.

They went over a cloverleaf and Omar saw a sign that said, "Welcome to Nassau County."

He knew that Lewis worked at an ambulance company somewhere in a place called Lawrence, which was located in a neighboring county. Perhaps that's where they were heading.

Lewis drove north on Route 878 and then made a left on Doughty Boulevard. He followed a car or two behind. He was sure by this time that Lewis did not know that he was being followed.

Soon, Omar saw a large parking lot filled with ambulances and a tall sign that read, "Hunter Ambulance." Under the name was a smaller sign that said, "EMT's, Drivers Needed, All Shifts."

Omar saw Lewis drive into the parking lot and park his car. Lewis took a utility bag out of the back seat of the car and went into the well-lit one-story building.

He followed.

When Omar got into the building, he saw Lewis `walk towards a large locker room on the left of the building. There was a reception desk with a middle-aged woman sitting behind it.

She looked up.

"What can I do for you," she asked.

"I see you need EMT's," he answered. 'I just got my license and would like to fill out an application."

"Sure," she answered, pulling a piece of paper from a vertical file on the side of her desk. "You can sit over there and fill it out, or you can take it home and return it," she said, motioning with her head to a desk and chair nearby.

Omar could see the locker room from the desk. He decided to

stick around. He sat down at the desk and pretended to fill out the application.

He glanced at the locker room and saw Lewis go into another, smaller room at the end of the locker room. Through the open door he could see him pick up what looked to be a large piece of metal.

His excitement rose. That had to be the piece of debris from 587 that Lewis put up for sale on E-Bay.

Lewis took the piece of metal and walked out of Omar's sight. In a minute of two, when he did not reappear, Omar figured that he had left the building by another exit.

"I'll bring this back later," he told the woman at the desk as he rushed from the building, just in time to see Lewis put the metal object in the back of an ambulance that was parked nearby the building.

Lewis got into the ambulance and pulled away, making a left turn on Burnside Avenue.

Omar got into his car and followed the ambulance.

Lewis drove back over the New York City Line, made a left turn at Mott Avenue and then a right turn at Beach 20 Street, a one way street that ran south to the beach and Wavecrest Gardens. In ten minutes, the Saudi could see that they were back on Seagirt Boulevard.

He followed Lewis to the rear of his apartment building. Lewis parked his ambulance near a fire door and looked around to see if anybody was watching. Then, he quickly took the piece of metal from the back of the ambulance and walked towards the rear door of his apartment building.

Omar slid a knife out of his pocket and opened it with an audible "click." He was quickly upon Lewis, grabbing the taller man around his throat, trying to cut the throat with his knife.

Lewis, however, was younger, quicker and stronger than Omar. He pushed him away and took a ragged swing at Omar's face, missing by a few inches.

"What, are you crazy, man," Lewis yelled, gasping for breath, afraid of what this lunatic with a knife could do to him if he got close enough. "I ain't got nothing worth stealing. Get away from me."

Omar, still grasping the knife, said nothing. His eyes glared as he came at Lewis once again.

This time, however, Lewis was ready for the rush. He grabbed Omar's right arm, pushing his hand and the knife back towards Omar's body.

The two men went down, rolling in the dirt at the rear of the apartment building, locked in a death grip. Both men sensed that the first one to break free would be the winner.

Lewis somehow understood that this was not a simple robbery, that Omar meant to kill him no matter what, and that thought gave him strength. He continued to push on Omar's knife hand until he felt some resistance. He pushed harder. He felt the resistance increasing as the knife entered Omar's body.

He pushed with all his strength and felt the knife go deeper into the Arab's body. A wetness spread out on his own chest. At first, he thought that he had been wounded, that he was bleeding. Then he realized that the blood he felt was ebbing from his opponent's body.

Lewis felt Omar go slack in his arms. He moved back and his assailant's body slipped to the ground, blood running out of his stomach in the area where the knife still stuck out of his body.

Lewis bent down and felt the man's carotid artery on his neck. He had done the same thousands of times at the scene of fires, shooting incidents and auto accidents. Somehow, however, this one was not real.

"Holy Shit," Lewis thought. "I killed him."

He had to decide what he was going to do next. He pushed the piece of wreckage inside the rear door, into the basement hallway. He quickly carried it to the bicycle storage room a few feet down the darkened hallway and pushed it behind some old, rusty bikes that had been abandoned for years.

He returned outside and went to the ambulance. He picked up the microphone that was hooked to the dashboard. He could get into some minor trouble for bringing the ambulance to his home, but it was not unheard for a driver to make a quick stop at home during a tour if he lived locally in order to get fresh clothes or to go to the bathroom.

It would work, he thought.

"Hunter Dispatch, this is 77 Charlie," he said into the microphone, his voice quaking.

"Hunter Dispatch," the radio dispatcher answered, her tone bored. "Go ahead 77 Charlie."

"You'd better send some cops to the rear of 20-47 Seagirt Boulevard, Dispatch. Some guy just jumped me with a knife and I think I wasted him. He's dead."

"Say again, 77 Charlie," the now wide-awake and astounded voice said.

"Just send the cops, man. Just send the cops."

Lewis sat down on the curb and waited for the patrol car to arrive. He had to figure out what had happened, what he was going to tell the cops when they showed up.

What could he tell them? He was not sure himself what had happened and why.

"Why did that guy want to kill me," he wondered. "What have I done that I deserve to be killed?"

VIII

B illy Droesch was tired and irritated. He had been up all night, assisting his fellow night watch detectives in catching a homicide in the neighboring 101 Precinct, a homicide that made no sense.

They had the killer, an ambulance driver who claimed that the murder was a case of self-defense. Billy would be inclined to accept that story from the killer if there were not so many questions about the incident.

First of all there were a number of major questions about the guy who was killed. He had no identification, no markings or labels in his clothing. His fingerprints came back negative from the FBI's archives as well as the New York State database.

Add to the fact that he was obviously Middle Eastern and it was two months after September 11, gave urgency to finding out who the dead man was and why he had tried to kill an ambulance driver with no criminal connections.

Secondly, there did not seem to be a motive for the dead man to attack the ambulance driver, let alone any other motive but self-defense for the driver to kill the unidentified man. There is always a motive, however. The television scripts had taught him that.

There had to be a reason for the dead man's attack on Lewis. Otherwise, it made no sense, he thought.

The whole thing was giving him a headache.

He had already run Lewis through all of the databases at his

97

disposal. The only hit he got was Lewis' application for EMT and his license. His fingerprints were on file and they proved that Lewis was who he said he was, but there was little doubt about that in the first place.

He decided to "Google" Lewis and see if anything turned up. He turned to his computer and double-clicked on his web browser. When it came up, he quickly typed "Google" into the URL line and then typed in Lewis' name. There were several hits.

There were a couple of newspaper articles from the local paper about his participation in responding to accidents and the program from his EMT graduation ceremony.

The last one, however, interested Droesch. Lewis had been active on E-bay and some of his feedback comments had found their way to other websites and then to Google.

He wondered if E-bay had some sort of weird connection to his case.

Droesch called the department's TARU unit. The acronym stood for Technical Assistance Response Unit, and they did all sorts of electronic work for the department. Within TARU was a computer unit made up of crack hackers.

One of them had gone to the academy with Droesch and they often had a beer and talked about the job and how it was changing.

The phone rang three times before it was picked up.

"TARU, PAA Simms," the voice said.

"Detective Droesch, 100 Squad. I need to talk with Elio Velez.

"One moment, Detective," the administrative aid responded.

He heard a few clicks and his old friend picked up.

"Velez."

"Hey, Elio, Tommy. I need a favor that involves some computer work."

"What do you need?"

Droesch explained what he needed and why.

"Spell the name for me, Billy. I got some time and I'll get back to you in a few hours. Should be able to do something if there's anything there to find."

Droesch carefully spelled out Lewis' name phonetically and hung up.

As he hung up, Ken Staller walked in. Staller parked his department car in the precinct's parking lot each day and was on the way to work. He often stopped in to speak with some of the people he knew when he was assigned to that precinct earlier in his career.

Staller grabbed a cup of coffee from the pot that was always brewing in the squad room on the precinct's third floor.

"This is a strange one, Ken," Droesch said. "Caught a homicide last night in the 101, up at Wavecrest Gardens. Some guy tried to mug or kill an ambulance driver and the driver wasted him. Says that it was self-defense and it looks that way. Right outside the guy's apartment building and everything, but it just don't smell right for some reason. The DOA is unidentifiable, Middle-Eastern, young, strong, in great physical shape. Why the hell did he mug an ambulance driver?"

"No way to trace him," Ken asked.

"No, but I'm running the perp. Nothing so far except that he has no record and goes on E-bay all the time."

"No crime to that. I use it myself."

"Just trying to touch all the bases. Don't even know where the ball is yet."

Staller laughed.

"Got the computer section at TARU looking into it," Droesch said. "See what turns up. Got to be something that caused this rag-head to attack an ambulance driver."

Just then the phone rang.

"Droesch, 100 Squad, Homicide," the detective said.

He listened intently for a few minutes, jotting notes in his notebook from time to time.

"Thanks, that's a big help," he said as he hung up.

Staller stared at him, as if to say "what?" "This gets even stranger," Droesch said. "You know what this guy was selling on E-bay. He was selling a piece of wreckage from Flight 587."

Staller got a chill. He knew immediately in his bones that there was a tie-in between that piece of wreckage and the killing. He told Droesch of his thoughts.

Obviously, Droesch agreed.

"Curioser and Curioser," the detective said. "Dorothy, we're not in Kansas anymore."

"What are you going to do now," Staller asked.

"Follow it up. See what that wreckage is and what it means. Talk to the victim again. See if anybody who bid on the piece of wreckage is now deceased. Lots to do."

He got up from his desk.

"Reach out if you get anything, will you Billy? This is getting really interesting. Are you going to pass this info on to the NTSB of the Feebees?"

"Not yet. Let's see what we got before we bring the feds into play."

Staller shook his head in agreement.

<hr/>

Sherry Holmes walked around the wreckage, now moved piece by piece to a large Hangar at Floyd Bennett Field. Holmes was the lead administrator for the NTSB's Go-team that responded to the AA 587 accident – and that is what she was ordered – and determined -- to call it.

Holmes did not know much about aircraft or about aircraft accidents. She had experts working for her that knew all that needed to be known. Even she had to admit, in her darkest hours, that she was a political appointee who had come up through the ranks as a press relation specialist for a number of companies in the airline industry, working first for National Airlines and then Eastern Airlines and TWA before moving on to work for Boeing in Seattle, Washington.

She eyed the aircraft. Even she could tell that there had been an explosion on the starboard side of the fuselage. She had her marching orders from above, however. What she had to do to serve her political sponsors and her former airline employers was to find a way to blame it on either the pilot or to mechanical failure.

That would not be hard to do. The real investigators worked for her and she had control of the evidence and could insure that nobody outside her control would get a close look at any of the wreckage that showed explosive damage.

That the tail and engines had fallen off could be blamed on G-Forces from wake turbulence, she had been told by experts, or from pilot error of some sort. There was always pilot error.

She smiled to herself. As long as she controlled the wreckage and controlled the experts, the world was hers and her

———≈«◑»≈———

While Droesch and Staller were still talking at the 100 Precinct in Rockaway, and Holmes was at Floyd Bennett Field, Reaza Mahobir was in Downtown Brooklyn, back on her regular beat, looking for stories about the Moslem community in New York City for a special section that Newsday was planning to run during the month of Ramadan.

While Reaza resented the fact that she was given this beat simply because she was both a woman and a Muslim, she liked working for Newsday and she knew that, if she kept generating good copy for her editors, she would get a chance at some real stories, stories like the crash of 587. She had turned out a fine piece on several women who had been impacted by both September 11 and the plane crash, thanks to the help of Ron Staller and his son, Ken.

She was going to enjoy dinner with the younger Staller, more than she liked to admit. He was an attractive man and very smart – for a police officer, she added to herself. She laughed. She really hoped that she would see him again, despite the fact that she never dated non-Moslems. Doing so was a dead end. Although she considered herself a modern woman, she would never get serious with somebody outside her faith. She had to admit, however, that Staller intrigued her and that she wanted to see more of him.

She found the address she was looking for, a Middle Eastern restaurant on Atlantic Avenue, nearby busy Court Street.

She was interviewing Palestinian women who owned or ran restaurants in that heavily-Arab section of Brooklyn. Most of their stories were mundane and so similar to each other that it seemed like they all came from the same mold. Perhaps they did. The woman took one look at her head covering and found it easy to tell their stories. That is what she and her editors had been counting on.

The last woman she interviewed for her story, however, was far different from the others with whom she had spoken. Proclaiming herself a "Palestinian Freedom Fighter," the woman bragged about how she had aided a "strike against the infidels" just a week ago.

When Reaza asked her what she had done, she became cryptic, saying only, "the devils fell from the sky because the praised martyrs made it do so, and that the whole world wound one day know what she knew and what she had done to further the Sheik's cause."

Reaza asked the women if she were talking about Flight 587 and the woman laughed.

"Go talk to Zeta Muhammad at the Eastern Crescent Restaurant," the woman said proudly. She can tell you a story that will make you proud of your faith."

So, Reaza was at the Eastern Crescent, looking for a story that was way outside her beat, but could easily get her some assignments in the metro side of the paper.

She entered the restaurant, empty now with the exception of a crew cleaning up for the lunch crowd and two Middle-Eastern men sitting at a table near the back door. Then, she noticed a woman sitting by herself nearby the kitchen. She wore a headscarf like Reaza, but her face was covered as well. All that showed were her eyes. She had a bottle of alcohol in front of her on the table, and a glass. Alcohol was strictly forbidden by the religion, and Reaza had never tasted alcohol although, as a journalist, she constantly saw what it did to others. In any case, many Moslems were secret drinkers, she knew. She quietly approached the woman.

"My name is Reaza Mahobir," she said to the woman, who looked up with little interest. "I'm a reporter for Newsday and I was told you might have a great story for me to report."

The woman looked unsure of herself, glanced over at the two men and stared at Reaza. It seemed to Reaza that she was making a decision about something, perhaps whether to speak with her or not.

"Not here," she said quietly. "Meet me in a half hour at the corner of Court and Livingston. I will talk with you in the open, not here."

She got up and walked out of the restaurant without another word, leaving Reaza to stare at her retreating back.

Reaza waited a moment and then followed. She walked around the neighborhood, looking in the windows of the many Arab-oriented shops, passing the headquarters of the PLO, the Palestine Liberation Organization. She did not take in much of what she was looking at, however. She was too busy working out a method of interviewing the woman she was about to meet, writing questions in her head.

She found herself glancing at her watch every five minutes until it was 25 minutes past the time she had left the restaurant. She turned right on Court Street and headed for Livingston Street, just down the block from the fabled headquarters of the New York City Board of Education and right around the corner from the city courts, probably one of the busiest street corners in New York City, outside of Manhattan.

She walked slowly, pacing herself, wondering what she was going to get from the mysterious woman.

"I shouldn't expect too much, then I won't be disappointed," she thought. "It's probably nothing, but it's worth the effort to find out."

She saw Zeata standing on the corner. If anybody could look furtive just standing on a street corner, her prospective informant did.

She worried that the woman would bolt as soon as she showed up, but she walked up to her.

"Zeata, my old friend," she said loudly. "I haven't seen you since high school. How have you been?"

The woman looked surprised, looked as if she were about to run, but she took the hint and answered, "Fine, and you?"

"Just great. We have so much to talk about, so many old times," Reaza said as she took the woman's arm and steered her away from the busy corner towards the old Abraham and Strauss Department Store, now long-closed but a more private site.

As they walked, Reaza asked, "Let's make this as quick and as comfortable as possible for both of us. What do you have to tell me?"

"I have to tell somebody," Zeata said. "I'm afraid that they will kill me because I know. I haven't slept since the plane came down. How do I know I can trust you to keep my name out of it? If you use my name, I will be dead before the day is gone. I would like to leave here and find someplace where I am not known, where I can be safe."

Reaza thought that Zeata was being overly dramatic, but she had to admit that people, particularly in the Arab community in New York, had been killed before for talking to either police officers or reporters.

"You have my absolute word that I will not use your name if I do the story," she answered as sincerely as she could. "The law protects me from disclosing my sources, even to the police."

Zeata looked a little less worried.

She was silent for a minute or more and Reaza thought that she had changed her mind about talking.

"I know who brought down that American Airlines plane," she blurted out suddenly, as if she were glad to finally get it out of her mouth.

"The government is saying that it's an accident," Reaza answered, a little surprised at the declaration. "How do you know it was brought down, that it wasn't an accident?"

"Because my friend, Tafiq, well, he's more than a friend... he told me how he and his friend shot it down from a boat with a shoulder-fired missile."

"Are you sure he was telling you the truth, not just making it up to impress you," Reaza asked, though she was fairly certain the woman was telling the truth.

"He showed me the missile he was going to use. There were two of them. They took a boat from a marina in Brooklyn, near the bay and went out into the bay near Rockaway and shot the airplane down."

"If this is true, it's a big story. How can I make sure that it is true? Is there anybody else who can corroborate your story — tell me that it is true. Do you have any proof?"

"No," Zeata said forlornly. "I have no proof, except that I rented the car that they used that day and I still have the papers from the rental place. I didn't want to leave them in the car because the plan was to abandon it in Brooklyn. Does that make me guilty of the crime?"

She was not sure.

"Probably not," she lied.

"Where are Tafiq and his friend now?"

"They have gone back to the Middle East. I'm not sure where. After Tafiq shot down the plane, he came back here for one last time and told me about his success. It was all over the news. Then we made love one last time and he headed out to Kennedy Airport. I haven't heard from him since. I think he'll be back soon for another attack."

Reaza was stunned. She had the story of the decade, but no proof. Even her editors would not print even such an important story without other corroborating sources. Especially when officials kept calling it an accident.

"Will you print my story," Zeata asked. "I am afraid that they will find me and kill me to keep me silent."

"I can't without checking further, without some other sources that insure that your story is true. I wish I could, but I can't without more facts, without some proof. My editors would never allow that."

Zeata pulled some papers from her pocket book and handed them to Reaza. It was the rental agreement for a Chevy Tahoe. Her signature was at the bottom of the forms.

Reaza told her new friend that she would investigate and that, if the story checked out, she would try and move her out of danger.

"Well, thanks for listening to me. Remember your promise if you ever do write the story. I do not exist."

Reaza shook her head as if to assure Zeata that she would always keep her promise.

"Where can I get in touch with you," Reaza asked.

Zeata gave her a cell phone number.

"Please don't use this unless you really have to," she said. "And please don't give it to anybody else."

Zeata turned and quickly walked away, heading back for the restaurant.

"What now," Reaza thought. "Who can I go to that might be able to corroborate her story?"

She immediately thought of Ken Staller. She was going to have dinner with him Friday night. Perhaps she could bring the conversation around to whether it was possible that flight 587 was brought down by a missile. Maybe he could add to her story, perhaps even corroborate it officially.

———————

Billy Droesch parked his department car on Crest Road and he and his partner, Richie Cohen took the slow elevator to Tommy Lewis' third floor apartment.

"You really think that Lewis has this piece of wreckage from flight 587 hid away in his apartment," Cohen asked. "Even if he does, why the hell would somebody want to kill him for it?"

"Won't know until we see it," Droesch replied. "Might not even know after we see it, but the department must have some experts that can answer that question. Nothing else makes any sense in this case."

They rode the elevator in silence to the fifth floor and walked to a door at the end of the long hallway. Droesch rang the doorbell.

"Who's there," came a voice from the other side of the door.

"Detective Droesch, police."

"What do you want?"

"Need to talk. Open the door."

"Do you have a warrant?"

"Only need to talk. Are you hiding anything inside that I need a warrant in order to come in, because I can get one based on your E-Bay sales."

That got his attention and Lewis opened the door.

"I told you, it was self-defense. Why do you keep bothering me?

"You're beginning to sound suspicious," Droesch said in his best detective voice. "Should I be suspicious?"

Lewis grumbled, but said, "come on in" and stood to one side as the detectives entered the small one-bedroom apartment.

Droesch looked around. There was nothing in view that looked like a piece of aircraft wreckage.

He decided to play it straight.

"Where's the aircraft wreckage," he asked. "We know all about it and believe that the piece of wreckage is the reason you were attacked."

Lewis looked like he swallowed a whole apple.

"What are you talking about," he said, stunned at the question.

"How does he know about the wreckage, and what difference does it make," Lewis thought. He decided that it didn't pay to screw around with the detective, especially when the detective might be able to pin a murder charge on him.

"What does it matter that I have wreckage from the airplane," Lewis asked. "Is that against the law?"

"Maybe, maybe not," Droesch answered, not even sure of the answer himself. That is something he should have checked out earlier.

"We have to check it out because it may prove once and for all that this guy tried to kill you and might provide us with a motive."

Lewis was confused. How could the piece of wreckage be the reason for the Middle Eastern man trying to kill him?

"It's in the basement. In the bicycle room," Lewis finally answered.

"Let's go take a look," Droesch said.

The three men rode the elevator to the basement and Lewis led them to a room at the end of the hall. He opened the door with a key and switched on the overhead light.

"It's in the back corner, behind those old bikes," Lewis said, pointing to the left corner of the large, relatively dark room.

"Damn it," he said silently to himself. "That thing was up to $250 and now I'm going to lose it to these cops."

Droesch and Cohen went back to the corner and dug out the piece of aircraft wreckage wedged behind the old bikes.

The two detectives had seen enough fires to know that the metal was burned and twisted.

"Did you take this from the crash scene itself," Droesch asked.

"No, a couple of blocks away. Never did get into the crash scene itself. It was leaning on a tree in a back yard about three blocks away. I think it was on 1-2-8, between Cronston and RBB."

"We're going to have to take this with us," Cohen said.

"Sure, why not," he said resignedly. "Better lose a couple of hundred bucks than wind up in prison."

"I think that this gets you off the hook," Droesch told Lewis. "I think that this is what the attacker was after."

"Why," Lewis asked, confused.

"I don't think he wanted anybody to ever see this metal," Droesch answered. "I think he wanted to bury both you and this metal before anybody could see it."

Droesch and Cohen took the wreckage to their car, but it was too big to fit either in the trunk or rear seat.

Droesch picked up his portable radio.

"100 Squad to central," he said.

"Central," a woman's voice answered.

"Is there a 100 or 101 van available to 85 us at Crest Road and Seagirt Boulevard for transportation of an object to the CSU base, central," he asked.

"101 Truancy Van One, Central," came another voice. "We were just going 98 after dismissal at PS 197 around the corner. We'll 85 the squad."

"Central, read direct," Droesch said and put the radio down on the car seat.

They would soon find out just why the attacker wanted that wreckage badly enough to kill for it, Droesch thought. He believed, however, that the man was a terrorist and that he already had his answer.

Ron Staller was getting ready to put the paper to bed. He checked the pockets of his shooing vest, looking to see if he had overlooked any photo disks or scraps of notes that he shoved in there as he was working a story in the field.

He came upon the seat belt fragment he had picked up near the crash site. He wondered if anybody else had found fragments of the aircraft and still had them. They might be important to investigators. In fact, he had a thought that he would get all of the witnesses who saw the plane in flames in the air and those who witnessed the actual crash together for a meeting to tell what they saw. The paper would invite the locals as well as the FAA, the FBI, the NTSB and the NYPD. He set out to set up the meeting at the Beach Club on the southern end of Beach 116th Street so he could get the notice into this week's paper. The owners of the bar-restaurant-catering hall were always willing to set up a public meeting gratis, and he was sure this time would be no different.

At the same time that Staller sat down to ready the next issue of the Beachcomber, a group of officials sat down at a large round table in the bowels of the White House in Washington, D.C.

While none of those at the meeting were present when American Airlines Flight 587 crashed in Rockaway, or were directly involved with the investigation into the crash, the decisions they were about to make would impact the investigation, the airline industry and the lives of several of those who were involved with the investigation.

Chairing the meeting was Thomas Paine, an amiable Texan who was the President's chief of staff and his closest political adviser.

He looked around the table at the diverse group of high-level officials who spread out at the table, waiting for him to tell them why they were there – although several could discern the purpose of the meeting simply by looking at which agencies and companies were represented.

To his right was Sherry Holmes, the NTSB's lead aviation investigator. Her subordinates would run the investigation. Next to Holmes was FBI Director Jim Morrison; then Attorney General Loretta Lyndon; Secretary of Transportation Joseph Fox; Admiral Gerald Miller, the secretary of defense; Penny Landis, the Secretary of Commerce; Jerome Fugate, the NYPD's chief of department and two company executives – John McGraw, a vice president at American Airlines and Renee Lafarge, a vice president with Airbus in Toulouse, France.

The rules for the meeting, the group was told, were that no staff were allowed and that no notes, transcriptions or recordings could be made. Secret Service agents from the president's detail had quickly and efficiently – albeit politely -- `checked each participant as he or she entered the room and would check them again on the way out. Cell phones and recording devices were confiscated, to be returned at the end of the meeting. What was going to be decided at the meeting – what had already been decided by the president and his closest advisors – was too sensitive to ever see the light of day.

Paine, a heavy-set ex-Texas legislator who had followed the president to the White House, would go back to his private sector position as CEO of a charter aviation company flying out of Love Field – a company with many government contracts.

He cleared his voice and set the tone of the meeting.

"You can guess why were are all here today, to get on the same page as regards American Airlines Flight 587," he began, nodding towards Holmes "The NTSB, thanks to Sherry, has already declared the crash as pilot error and that should be the tone and track that we all take moving forward. That decision has been vetted at the highest level of government and, for many reasons, some economic and some necessary for the defense of the homeland, and for national security reasons, that decision must be followed by every agency in the room."

Jerome Fugate, the only person in the room in uniform, looked pained, but he knew he had to make a point, even if it were rebuffed. It was cover your ass time and he wanted to be able to say that he had made his point if the whole cover-up went south.

He spoke up, knowing that he had to choose his words carefully. He was not about to give away what his detectives had found, or even that they had found anything that would change the decision to call it pilot error. He only knew that some top men and women under his command were working hard, long hours on the case and that they were not going to drop it without a fight.

"I would be remiss here, if I did not point out that my detectives are still working the case and that there is some preliminary evidence that the cause might be other than pilot error. There are a lot of questions, a lot of eyewitnesses who saw the plane on fire in the air, a lot of debris scattered around, including the tail and engines, in places they would not normally be if the crash resulted from pilot error. Why don't we wait until they have completed their report before we declare this a pilot error incident?"

"The NTSB will take care of all those questions," Paine retorted. "What you have to do is rein in your detectives to make sure they do not develop any evidence that proves any other outcome but pilot error."

"That might be hard to do. These are experienced, careful detectives, who have been working the case for a week. If I pull them off the case, tell them it's closed, it's not going to go over well and some of the information they find might get out to the public or even to the press. You're talking about multiple homicides and that's hard even for the White House to sweep that many deaths under the rug. Some of the best cops and the best investigative journalists in the country are working the story."

Paine looked angry and was about to speak when Holmes chirped in.

"We have all the evidence sealed in a hangar at Floyd Bennett Field," she said. "We are working to get all of the small residue that was scattered around the community and we are confident we will do just that. There is no evidence outside that hanger that shows any explosive residue on the plane. We will control the investigation and the final report, which will show that the first officer, who was flying the plane that day, overused the rudder after hitting wake turbulence and caused the tail to fall off the plane."

"I saw an interview with the head of the pilot's union on CNN yesterday, and he said that building a plane where the tail falls off when the pilot over-flies the rudder is like building a car where the wheels fall off every time the driver hits the brakes too hard. I don't think story about pilot error is going to fly," Fugate said.

"We'll handle the union and everybody else," Holmes said angrily.

Fugate was silent. H was a long-time political warrior, and knew when to back down – at least for now in this company.

"Let's go once around the table," Paine said. "Comments, ideas, reasons why we can't do this."

He pointed at Morrison.

"We will declare the crash an accident and close out the NYPD's involvement. That will give Chief Fugate cover to pull his detectives off the case immediately," Morrison said. "We all understand the need to keep this close, the make the terrorist angle go away. After 9-11, if the people find out that there is even a possibility that this is a terrorist act, the airline industry is toast and so is the U.S. economy. There is no up-side for this country in allowing a terroristic cause in this case."

He sat back in his chair.

Lyndon, a long-time Texas judge, went next.

"If nobody brings the Justice Department evidence of another cause, we will take the advice of the NTSB and FBI and drop any criminality issue."

Miller said, "This is not a defense issue. I don't even know why I am here today. If the president wants this, let's get it done. I vote for Tom's plan. Declare it pilot error, cut out the NYPD and let the NTSB do its thing."

"I can't imagine what would happen of the flying public found out that another airliner had been brought down by terrorists," Joseph Fox said. "It would stop all passenger flights, all cargo flights. The airlines would go out of business one by one, starting with American Airlines, and then the airplane manufacturers like Boeing and Airbus wouldn't be far behind."

Both McGraw and Lafarge looked up, pained at the possibility of what would happen to their stock portfolios if the truth got out.

They both shook their heads in agreement. Both spoke up, adding that everything they wanted to say had already been said by others, and that they preferred to stay out of the conversation.

Penny Landis agreed, saying, "I think we have a consensus. Chief, put an immediate hold on your detectives. We need to contain this, for the good of the country and the good of the country's businesses."

Paine adjourned the meeting and the participants filed out of the room, stopping to be searched by secret service agents on the way out.

Fugate was last to go.

"Jerry, a minute please," Paine said, sounding angry at what had just transpired..

The chief turned around and went to the head of the table where Paine remained seated.

"Are you on board with this," he asked Fugate. "Your cooperation and that of the PC is critical. This is a matter of national security and the orders come right from the top. Get it done and get it done immediately. I expect to see the PC announce the end of the department's involvement with the investigation by end of business tomorrow. Understood?

Without a word in response to the warning, Fugate turned and walked out of the room.

The PC might make some sort of bullshit statement that made it look as if the department was dropping the investigation at the direction of the FBI and NTSB, but he wasn't going to pull his detectives off the case yet. He was not going to allow the NYPD he had worked for over three decades take the fall for White House functionaries when the shit hit the fan and the cover-up went south, as he was sure it would. In fact, he was going to give his detectives full rein and allow the investigation to run its course, even if he had to keep the real investigation from the feds – something that was often done at One Police Plaza.

IX

Ken Staller was nervous about his first actual date with Reaza. In fact, he was not even sure that it was a date. He was surprised at his feelings. He had been with a number of women in his life, married to one for a few years and had even lived with another for a few months. Yet, he felt that there was something special about Reaza. Perhaps it was her exotic look, the clothing she wore so well, and her profession as a journalist. There certainly was something special about her, more special than he cared to admit because of the short time he'd known her and the difference in their religions, their cultures.

He had asked her to dinner at the recently-reopened Lightship Restaurant on the next block, just east of the crash site, and she had readily accepted. His first thought was that she had some feelings for him, at least fledgling feelings. He knew that he would like to get to know her better. Deep down, however, he was sure that she just wanted to meet with him only as a source close to the flight 587 investigation. Reporters were always cultivating sources, particularly in the law enforcement community, and he might simp ly be another source to the beautiful Moslem woman.

Now, sitting at a table at the Lightship, he had convinced himself that he was nothing more than a source, but he saw no other way to find out but to let it play out.

The restaurant was crowded, although it was in the greatly-reduced "frozen zone" around the crash site. Locals were trying as hard as they could to return to normalcy, streets were cleaned, stores reopened, crime scene tape removed, lots of people in the streets, some just taking a walk, others drawn to the crash scene by the wall-to-wall media coverage the past few days. No cars were allowed into the area with the exception of emergency vehicles, but people could walk in to use the stores on Beach 129th Street or the restaurant, on the corner of Beach 130th Street and Newport Avenue.

Through the front window of the restaurant, Ken could see at least two burned-out skeletons of homes and three empty lots where homes once stood.

All of the bodies had been removed from the area days earlier and what remained of the homes where the plane had crashed had been demolished that day. The others were scheduled to be demolished early the next week. What was left of the aircraft itself had been moved to a hangar at Floyd Bennett Field in Brooklyn, although federal investigators continued to search the streets and backyards for pieces of the plane.

Ken had asked Droesch if he could get into the hangar to take a look at the damage, but the detective told him angrily that he, himself, could not get in to the hanger even though he was the lead detective. It seems that the feds had blocked access to everybody but the NTSB and FBI agents who still swarmed the area. That seemed suspicious to both Droesch and Staller, but there was little they could do except to keep asking.

All the talk at the restaurant was about the crash, about people who had not been home but had lost everything they owned, of people who had left their homes minutes before the plane struck to run errands, to go to work or to deliver their children to some sort of activity.

The conversations also centered on the five people in the community who had died. There was an older couple, a young man whose best friend had died two months earlier in the north tower of the WTC, a woman with children. After losing 70 community members in the attack on the World Trade Center, another five seemed to be an added and incredible burden to the west end community.

Ken was so engrossed in the scene outside the window that he did not see Reaza walk up to the table where he was sitting.

"It's really devastating," isn't it," Reaza asked. "Especially for people who live around here."

Ken looked up and smiled.

"Hi, didn't see you come in. Yeah, it's devastating. It's also a miracle that more people weren't killed. You have to think that the first officer who was flying the plane saved lots of lives by spiraling it straight in rather than gliding in and taking out dozens of homes."

Reaza gracefully slid into the booth opposite Ken.

He couldn't help but notice how beautiful she was, how feminine. "Don't get your hopes up," he thought to himself. "She's all business."

"Would you like a drink," he asked.

"I'd like something non-alcoholic," she answered. "A diet Coke would be nice."

"Boy, am I stupid. I forgot that Moslems don't drink alcohol," he answered quickly, sure that he was losing points rapidly.

Reaza, however, just laughed.

"No problem," she said with a smile. "Lots of people don't drink, but you can if you want."

The waitress came to their table, bringing some menus and Ken ordered a beer and a diet Coke. She left and both Ken and Reaza looked at their menus.

"What's good here," Reaza asked.

Ken was not sure that she could eat. He should have researched the dietary habits of Moslems before he came to the restaurant. He tried to play it safe.

"The steak is good," he answered. "The fish is usually fresh."

Reaza leaned over and touched his hand as if to reassure him that everything was all right. She smiled at him once again. Her touch left him breathless for a second, but he quickly recovered.

"I think I'll have the steak," he said, to cover up his nervousness.

"The salmon special looks good. I'll have that with mashed potatoes and broccoli," she said.

Ken relaxed. At least that was out of the way.

Ken signaled for the waitress and she came over and took their orders.

"This looks like a nice neighborhood place," Reaza said, making small talk.

"The owner is Jimmy Bechtold, an ex-firefighter who lost his son at the World Trade Center," Ken said. "Then, just two months later, a plane crashes across the street from his restaurant."

"Poor man," she said, shaking her head, but making a mental note to see if there was a story there.

The two made small talk until the food came and then they ate in silence. When they were finished, Reaza said, "That was good. Do you come here often?"

"A couple of times each month," he answered.

"On dates," she asked.

He blushed. "My job doesn't allow me lots time or opportunity to meet women, or for dates for that matter."

He was glad that she didn't ask him if he were married because he did not want to have to explain to her what happened between him and his ex.

"You're here with me, and it's nice," Reaza answered, touching his hand once again.

"Is this a date," he asked, laughing, "Or an interview."

"Definitely a date," she said after a second's thought.

"That's good," he answered. "I was beginning to wonder."

"Can I come over and sit next to you for coffee," he asked. "Seeing that this is a date."

Now, it was her turn to blush.

"That would be nice."

Ken floated out of the booth and went around to sit next to Reaza, who slid over to make room for him.

The two looked at each other and something passed between them. She smiled. The waitress came and they both ordered coffee and dessert. They made small talk while they waited for the coffee and desert to come, both aware that a line had been crossed.

He moved towards her and kissed her quickly on her lips. She responded immediately.

"Not here," she said. "Everybody knows you."

Ken moved back, aware that Reaza was right, but it took all of his will power to do so.

They drank their coffee and ate their desert quickly, and the waitress brought the check. Ken paid and the two walked out into the darkness. Reaza's hand slipped into Ken's, and their fingers entwined. He decided to take a chance. Never up, never in.

"Would you like to go to my place for some more coffee," Ken asked. "It's only two blocks away."

"That sounds good," she said.

They walked in silence, holding hands.

On beach 129th Street they turned south, towards the beach and walked up the beach block.

"It must be great so live so close to the ocean," Reaza said.

Ken grunted a "yes," as he took his key from his pocket and fumbled with the lock. They went in. Reaza took off her coat and looked around the small one-bedroom apartment.

"Nice," she said.

"I'm not here too often," Ken answered. "Don't be surprised if it's bit of a mess." Ken walked over to Reaza and put his arm around her. He kissed her softly.

She responded to his kiss, moving her body closer to his and putting her arms around his neck. He dropped his hands down to her rear end, fondling both hemispheres and then pulling her towards him. He felt himself get hard. She moaned, moving one hand from around her neck to his crotch, fondling his penis.

He moved his hand from her rear end, bringing it up to her breast, fondling it softly and then removing her head scarf and kissing her neck. His hands moved to her blouse. He began unbuttoning the smooth buttons.

She undid his belt and then pulled down on his zipper.

He had her blouse undone and she allowed him to slip it off over her smooth shoulders. He fumbled with her bra, opening it and releasing her breasts. The bra dropped to the floor as he bent down and kissed her nipples, allowing his tongue to pass over the hardened brown orbs.

She moaned again, responding to his touch. She moved away from him, kicking off her shoes and undoing her skirt. The skirt dropped to the ground and her pantyhose followed in quick order. While she was doing that, Ken took off his shoes and his pants.

They faced each other, nude.

She came into his arms and they kissed longingly, their tongues touching and then moving away. They moved into the small bedroom. Reaza laid down on the bed and Ken moved next to her. The embraced and rolled over each other.

Ken alternately fondled her rear end and her breasts as she took hold of his penis and moved it towards her vagina.

Ken kissed her forehead, her nose, her throat, each of her breasts, her belly button and then moved down to her vagina, kissing her and running his tongue over her uvula.

They pressed against each other and Reaza took Ken's penis and brought it nearby her vagina.

He entered her gently, pressed down and began to pump.

Reaza brought her legs up around Ken's waist. They moved together and finally climaxed together.

"I love the feel of you inside me," Reaza said.

"I could stay here all night," he answered, breathing hard.

"I could use that coffee you promised me," she said with a laugh.

Ken rolled over and went to make the coffee. Reaza followed him into the kitchen, moving close and putting her arms around his still-nude waist. He turned and kissed her hard. She responded. He began to get hard once again.

"Want to go back into the bedroom," he asked.

"I guess the coffee can wait," she said.

She took his hand and led him back to the bed. This time was slower, more erotic for both of them. The lust was gone, but the feelings remained. When they both had orgasms nearly at the same time for a second time, Ken got up.

"I'll go finish the coffee," he said. "You'd better stay here or we'll never get any coffee tonight," he said, laughing.

Reaza threw the pillow at him and then rolled over on the bed, smiling. Ken went into the kitchen and finished making the coffee. He put two mugs on the table, some milk and sugar. He called to Reaza to come into the kitchen. A minute later, she did so. She had the cover sheet from the bed wrapped around her body.

"Isn't it a little late to be modest," Ken asked.

"It's indecent to drink coffee while nude," she answered.

He walked over to her and kissed her. Their tongues danced.

Then, he went back to the stove and poured the coffee into the two mugs.

Reaza pulled one over to herself and poured in some milk from the container. She sipped contentedly. They drank the coffee in silence for a minute or two.

"Are you involved with the crash investigation at all," Reaza asked.

"Not really," he said. "Do we do the interview now that we got the other thing out of the way?"

She laughed. "No, just curious."

"The NTSB says that it's an accident, so the investigation has slowed down, I guess. I am friendly with the detective who caught the case and there are a couple of loose ends he's looking at, like a homicide that might have been tied somehow to the crash, but that's all."

"Has the name Shafiq come up at all, do you know?"

Ken was suddenly interested, his sexual interest diminished and his police radar on full alert.

"Not that I know of. Why?"

"I met this Arab woman in Brooklyn when I was nosing around the Muslim community on Atlantic Avenue who says that her boyfriend, this Tafiq person, claimed to have been involved in bringing the plane down," she said. "Apparently, he's gone back to the Middle East."

Reaza told Ken the story of the strange meeting with Zeata Muhammad. Ken listened intently.

"Do you mind if I pass that on to the detectives tomorrow morning," Ken asked.

"If you tell me about the homicide that might be connected to the crash," she answered.

Ken talked and Reaza listened.

"The guy who got killed might be connected to the crash," Reaza said finally. "He was trying to kill the person who had a piece of the wreckage because he didn't want anybody to see it. That's the only thing that makes any sense."

Ken thought for a minute. "And he didn't want anybody to see the piece of wreckage because it showed evidence of terrorist activity," Ken said thoughtfully. It all ties together, except for the fact that the NTSB and the FBI have looked at lots of wreckage and they say there was no evidence of explosion or fire.

"Maybe they're running a cover-up of the real reason for the crash," she said.

Ken just nodded his head. His thoughts exactly.

"Can I take a shower before I leave," Reaza asked.

Ken smiled. "Maybe we can save water and take a shower together," he answered. Reaza smiled and walked to the small bathroom, which housed a stall shower. Ken followed her, pulling some towels and two washcloths from a hall closet. He turned on the water and adjusted it until it was just right, setting the shower head to a fine spray. Without a word, the two stepped under the water. With her back to Ken, she asked him to scrub her back. He did, and then slowly worked his way down to her rump, lathering it up and then stepping back to let the water run the soap away. Then he reached around her and worked his was slowly from her neck down her body to her breasts and her legs. When he was done, he turned around and Reaza slowly worked her way around his body. When they were both done, she turned to face him and they kissed for a long time, their tongues moving in tandem. She pushed him away and walked out of the shower stall, rubbing her body with one of the plush towels that hung on a wall holder.

"I'd better get going," Reaza said suddenly. "It's late and I have to work in the morning."

The two got dressed and Ken walked Reaza back to her car. They kissed passionately.

"I'll call you tomorrow," Ken said.

"You'd better," Reaza said as she slipped behind the wheel.

—⇒«(◆)»⇐—

While Ken and Reaza were sharing a bed in Ken's apartment, Billy Droesch was at his desk, making some much-needed calls before signing out for the night. One of those calls was to the Medical Examiner's office.

He identified himself and asked for the cause of Omar's death. The switchboard operator transferred him to the duty ME, a woman named Joan Connelly, who Droesch knew well.

"Hi, Billy," she answered. "What can I do for you?"

"I need the COD and autopsy report on that middle eastern gentleman who was killed in Far Rockaway."

"Just a minute." He heard the shuffling of paper.

She came back on.

"Strange. The case has been marked "National Security, eyes only," and the body has apparently been transferred to the Saudi Embassy for transshipment to Saudi Arabia. Sorry, I can't help you."

"Did you see the report?"

"No, Gina Cromarti did the post and she went on a surprise vacation for a few weeks earlier today. Can't help you."

He hung up. One more mystery to add to the building house of cards that the case had become. He decided to call it a night and pick it up tomorrow, wondering if the body had gone to Saudi Arabia and where the debris from the crash that he had tried to kill for might wind up.

X

Jim DiGreggorio stood in front of Hanger 5 at Floyd Bennett Field, enjoying the Saturday morning quiet and drinking the first of several cups of coffee he expected to drink that day. The 70-year-old former Navy Chief Aviation Machinist's Mate spent most of his weekend days at the hanger as the volunteer supervisor for the national park's HARP – Historic Airplane Reconstruction Project. He and other volunteers, most of whom would be showing up shortly, were currently restoring a Vietnam-era A-4 Skyhawk, what was called a "Scooter" in his active duty days during the Vietnam War and beyond. In fact, the great majority of the volunteers lovingly restoring the attack aircraft, a model similar to the one flown by John McCain, were former military or civilian aircraft mechanics and airframe engineers.

To the left of Hanger 5 was the NYPD's headquarters of the department's Emergency Services Unit and the Aviation Unit. To the far right was the city's sanitation training base. Directly ahead was a hanger that once was a technical training building during the time the field was better known as Navy Air Station, New York and which the NTSB was using to recreate the airliner that crashed into Rockaway earlier in the week. He has seen his share of aircraft accidents both from war and peacetime activities and was anxious to take a look at what remained of the Airbus A-300.

Problem was, the hanger that housed the aircraft was guarded by heavily-armed federal marshals, an unusual event even for the military, but unheard of in the civilian world. Nobody was allowed into the hangar except for NTSB and federal police officials. He wondered why.

He had become friendly with one of the marshals, a younger man who had also been in naval aviation, a former Aviation Boatswain Mate, but even that friendship could not buy him into the hanger. His new friend said that they had strict orders to keep everybody out. There had been some problem earlier in the week when a New York Times reporter and photographer team had showed up to see the wreckage but they were quickly turned away and told never to come back.

He certainly was interested in the crash, being a Rockaway resident, and perhaps he could find out something more when he attended the meeting hosted by the local newspaper to be held at the Beach Club on Monday night.

＝➤«(◉)»◅＝

Ken Staller got up on Saturday morning sure of two things – that he was really attracted to Reaza and that he had to talk as early as possible to Billy Droesch. He called the squad, but the detective was "in the field." Staller asked the desk to reach out to Droesch and have him call Staller's cell phone "forthwith," which in cop-speak meant that it was really important and needed to be done immediately.

Five minutes later, his cell phone rang.

"Staller," he answered

"Hi, Ron. It's Billy. Got your message. I was going to call you in a few minutes anyway. Something strange, that wreckage we took off the Lewis guy, it's gone. Seems our guys called the feds about some questions they had and ten minutes later two FBI guys came and took the piece away, along with all the DD-5's and the other reports and notes about how we got it and what we found."

"What did they find?"

"Don't know, and they won't tell me. The feds said that it was "national security" and told our lab guys that they would be arrested for treason if they ever talked about it. This case is getting stranger and stranger."

And, to add to that, he added, the body of the man killed by tommy Lewis in self-defense has disappeared, shipped to the Middle East, recovered by the Saudi government."

"I need to talk to you face to face," Staller said. "I have some interesting information, and the fact that the feds are still in the case when they say they are not, makes what I have even more interesting. Can you meet me at the Sherwood Diner in Inwood in an hour? I'd rather not do this in Rockaway."

"You're making this sound like a spy thriller," Droesch responded. "You're making me wonder where this is going. I'll be there in a little over an hour."

———— ⊶«◉»⊷ ————

Jim DiGreggorio wanted to eat in peace and quiet and the noisy grinding machines running inside Hanger 5, where there was a small break room, made that all but impossible, so he took his bag lunch outside in the clear, but cool Saturday afternoon. He walked towards the bay and sat on a bulkhead, looking first toward the looming Marine Parkway Bridge and then towards Rockaway.

He heard a loud noise, a large truck changing gears as he came to a stop nearby the guarded NTSB hangar. The tarp that wrapped the flatbed's cargo was loose at one end and had folded up to stick to something on the top of the load.

The truck's driver got out, took a clipboard off the front seat next to him and walked to the secure hangar. The truck was between DiGreggorio and the hanger and the driver was lost from sight. The vet could see part of the load under the tarp and he could see that it was part of an aircraft fuselage, with a door and a row of windows clearly visible.

He had seen enough aircraft upsets to know that the fuselage had been hit with some sort of shrapnel that ripped it like a tin can, forcing the aluminum inward towards the cabin. The black explosive residue was clear to anybody who has seen such damage before – and he had seen it plenty of times.

DiGreggorio felt his body shiver. He had been following the story of AA 587 closely and had read in the New York Times that morning that the incident had been declared an accident by both the NTSB and the Governor. He knew with surety that what he was looking at was not the result of an accident. He wished he had a camera, but his was in the trunk of his car, 100 yards away. Just then the driver came back to the truck, mounted up and moved it through the doors of the hanger, which now stood open. He threw the rest of his unfinished lunch into a nearby trash barrel and walked back inside HARP.

It was not a good idea to be caught looking too closely at the truck with its cargo. Not good at all. Something was going on and he didn't like it or want to be part of it.

———◦((◦))◦———

Ken Staller pulled his car off Rockaway Turnpike in Lawrence, Long Island, into the parking lot for the Sherwood Diner and saw the two detectives standing at the top of the ramp that ran to the front door. They all went inside and asked for a table in the back room, figuring they would have more privacy away from the majority of diners in the large front room.

Ken started by telling them what Reaza had told him the night before, referring to his notebook when he needed a fact he couldn't recall. The two detectives pulled out notebooks of their own to record what they were told.When Ken told them about the rental car, they interrupted his narrative to ask where she had rented it and under what name.

Ken looked at his notes and told them.

Billy held up his hand to stop Ken and took out his cell phone. He hit a number saved in the phone and passed the information over to somebody at the other end.

"Should have something in a few minutes," he said.

The three men waited, absentmindedly eating their breakfasts. Droesch's phone rang and he picked it up while the others waited for him to finish the call.

"Got it," Billy said, turning his phone off. The car was rented on Monday for two days. It went missing when it wasn't returned on time, so the agency put out a stolen vehicle report. Last night, federal park service police officers spotted it abandoned at the Barren Island Marina on Jamaica Bay, across Flatbush Avenue from Floyd Bennett Field. The cops are going to meet us there in an hour. I'm going to arrange for a department tow to pick it up and bring it in to our shop for crime scene to pull it apart."

"Makes sense," Cohen said. "That's probably where they took off from to get out into Jamaica Bay It' only a short run from there to where the plane was hit. I guess they dropped the boat off somewhere else, probably somewhere near public transportation. We'll have to check to see what kind of boat it was and then look for it in other marinas around the bay."

The Barren Island Marina was only a half hour away on the Belt Parkway, so the three police officers finished their breakfast while Ken finished telling them what he had learned from his informant. Then they paid the bill and took off in Droesch's department car for the Belt Parkway and Flatbush Avenue. They all understood that the abandoned rental car could lead them to identifying the men who brought down American Airlines Flight 587 and perhaps even those who ordered them to do it.

Twenty-five minutes later, the two cars pulled off the Belt Parkway onto Flatbush Avenue South and then right into the marina parking lot. At the far end of the lot stood two Federal Park Police patrol cars. Four men in uniform, one apparently a senior officer, stood by their cars. Nearby, a few feet from the police cars, stood an SUV encircled by yellow crime scene tape.

The Parks officer walked towards them.

"You must be PD," he said, "I'm inspector Ian McConnell, parks police. We secured the car, and it's all yours whenever you want it. We checked with the guy who owns the concession. He told us there was a boat that left here on Monday morning and the mooring was paid for until Wednesday, but it left on Tuesday morning and never came back. We checked marinas in the area, and the boat turned up moored in Howard Beach, not far from your Harbor Adam dock. We've got somebody watching it."

"Thanks for the help. I'll get somebody from the 106 squad to take a look. Do you know who it's registered to," Droesch asked.

McConnell pulled out his notebook, ripped out the last page and handed it to Droesch. The name on the paper was Middle Eastern and the address was in Howard Beach, not far from where the boat was found.

They all stood around for an hour waiting for the NYPD tow truck to remove the car. Droesch signed the custody form for the federal police and the car was towed away.

"As I see it, we have a couple of leads to check out," Droesch said. "We have the woman who rented the car and who says her boyfriend shot down the plane with a missile launcher, the boat owner in Howard Beach, the fact that both the used and unused launchers may be on the bottom of the bay somewhere, and the fact that a piece of the wreckage was taken from the NYPD by the feds and we can't track it down

Droesch looked his notes and told Ken that he and his partner would take him back to the diner to retrieve his car and then they were on the way to Howard Beach to check out the boat and its owner and to Brooklyn to check out Reaza.

They hoped the leads would not evaporate like the Wavecrest Garden lead did just days ago.

"Keep me in the loop," Ken said. "My dad's newspaper is hosting a witness meeting at the Beach Club on Beach 116th Street on Monday night. I'm going to be there. Might be some interesting people to speak to. It might pay for you to be there as well. I understand he's invited the feds, and maybe we can get some information from them. In any case, there will certainly be lots of locals who saw the plane in the air and some who picked up debris and have been asked to bring it to the meeting. I hear that the first officer's father is coming from Connecticut. It certainly won't be a waste of your time."

Ken walked back to his car, pondering the myriad of questions the case generated. He was not a detective, but he was brought up to be questioning and proactive. His police training had magnified those skills.

There were just too many unanswered questions, too many questions, too many disappearing artifacts.

He decided that he would discuss them with his father and see what he thought and perhaps with Reaza, who he wanted to see again as soon as possible, for reasons of his own that had nothing to do with AA 587.

XI

R on Staller was miffed. No, he was pissed. Despite his best efforts, both the NTSB and the FAA were blowing off his witness meeting. No reason for us to come, he had been told, because eyewitnesses are typically unreliable. Both of the federal agencies told Staller that they already had all the witness statements they needed. None of the officials were interested in listening to eyewitnesses tell about what they allegedly saw.

In addition, he had contacted all the daily papers that had been covering the crash and each of them had told him that their aircraft beat writers were busy elsewhere, at an industry convention in Dallas, where a new breed of quieter aircraft engines would be announced. To the editors, that was more important than listening to some locals fanaticize about what they had seen.

He thought the meeting he had called was important, but none of the officials or the media seemed to think so.

The meeting was called for 7:30 p.m., He looked at his watch. The meeting was about an hour away and the Givens brothers, who owned the Beach Club restaurant, which stood about 30 feet from the boardwalk as well as the Sunset Diner, has set up a table and a few dozen chairs in what was usually the room where the pre-dinner cocktail hour was held in the catering hall cum restaurant. Staller hoped that, at very least, the seats would be filled with locals.

One bright point of the evening was a call from Stan Shades, the pilot father of Carl Shades, who was coming from his Connecticut home to the meeting. As a long-time airline pilot he could add some expertise to the meeting lacking any other experts and Shades said that he was concerned with the preliminary results of the investigation, which seemed to say that it was his son's flying skills, or lack thereof, that had caused the tail to separate from the plane and therefore caused the crash.

The elder Shades told Staller that he wanted to have informal discussions with some of the eyewitnesses to get his own take on the crash.

Rob Givens walked out of the back room and approached Staller.

"Do you want some tables set up for people to deposit any wreckage they found after the crash, he asked. "I have some and I know that others picked up odds and ends."

"Good idea," Ron said. "Put it over there by the door so that people can see it when they walk in. Thanks for all your help on this."

"No problem," Rob said. "Glad to help."

He walked back through the rear door and a minute later two kitchen workers brought out two trestle tables and set them up near the door. One of them held a sign and some scotch tape. On one of the tables, he taped a sign that said "Have some debris to share with the meeting, this is the place for it."

The two left and quickly came back with a box of material, taking it out of the box and putting it on the table. He walked over and took a look. One piece of debris looked familiar, the twin to the gray seatbelt he had picked up and put into his shooting vest the day of the crash. In fact, it looked to be the other half of the piece he had. He walked to his car in the parking lot and took his piece of wreckage out of the pocket of his vest and put it next to Given's piece. They joined perfectly.

To his untrained eye, the two pieces of webbed belt looked as if they had been pulled apart by a great force and were stained by a black residue. He wondered again how the official version of the cause was that there were no outside forces exerted on the aircraft before it hit the ground.

By 7:15, a number of locals had come into the room and seated themselves. Many of them had spent time looking at the growing pile of debris from the crash that had been deposited on a table near the door.

Ken Staller walked in, talking with Ed Lopat, the NTSB investigator who he knew previously from his NYPD position and who he had met in the parking lot.

"My father told me that you guys weren't coming to the meeting," Staller said. "I'm surprised to see you."

"I'm not here, at least not officially," Lopat answered, but not convincingly or enthusiastically. "The official investigation is really over – pilot error. I'm just another civilian looking for some insight into what the eyewitnesses saw before and after the crash."

"I'm going to look for my father," Staller said. "I'd like to talk to you after the meeting and see what you have to say – unofficially, of course."

Lopat wandered over to the table now laden with wreckage. Just another civilian, he wandered down the length of the two tables, picking up pieces of debris and studying them before putting them back down. A few times he looked closely at one piece or another and then shook his head before moving on.

He walked to a seat in the last row, certain that he would have to be careful in dealing with the information he had just learned by looking at the debris on the tables. He had no doubt that it had come from AA 587 and less doubt that it showed an explosive residue.

Ken Staller found his father talking with an older man. His father spotted him and introduced the other man.

Stan Shades, this is my son, Ken, who is an NYPD sergeant," he said. "Ken, this is Stan, Carl Shade's father, who has come from Connecticut to join us tonight."

Ken knew exactly who Shades was and was glad to meet him.

"Hi, Mr. Shades," Ken said. "Glad you could make it. Hope you learn something that will help you to clear your son's reputation."

"Thanks," Shades said. "I think that I already have something. I was a pilot for 35 years and did some Green Board investigations when I was in the Navy, and I know explosive residue when I see it, and it's all over the debris that you have sitting on those tables in the back of the room. Safeguard that stuff, it's liable to be valuable for the investigators, but I don't think that they'll be too interested in anything that disproves their contention that my son flew the tail off the plane."

Shades referred to the information that the NTSB was pushing unofficially that his son reacted too aggressively to wake turbulence from the JAL heavy in front of him and his aggressive use of the rudder literally tore the tail and the two engines from the plane.

While they were speaking to each other, Ken glanced towards the door and saw Reaza Mahobir walk in. His heart leaped a bit, but he tried to maintain his professionalism. He hadn't seen her for a few days and definitely wanted to talk to her again. He saw her walk towards the displayed wreckage and he thought of going to join her at the table.

But first, he wanted to find out what Shades meant about "having something" about the accident after looking at the wreckage brought in by the locals and why he thought it was valuable to the investigators.

"What do you mean, what did you see on the debris at the rear of the room? He asked.

"I spoke to some of the people who brought that stuff in, and most of it was found blocks from the crash scene. A lot of it shows evidence of some sort of explosion and that explosion didn't happen after the place crashed. It was thrown from the plane long before it hit the ground. To my mind, it proves that the plane was falling apart long before it hit the ground and that means damage in the air."

Ken glanced around the room for Ted Lopat. He found him talking to some locals near the door.

"See that guy in the blue sport jacket near the door," he told Shades. "Go talk with him. I think he'll be interested in what you have to say."

Shades said thanks and moved off to introduce himself to Lopat, still not knowing that he worked for the NTSB. Staller hadn't told him because he was not sure that Lopat wanted to be identified as being at the meeting.

Ken excused himself from his father and started walking towards Reaza when he saw Billy Droesch and Richie Cohen walk in.

He walked over to the detectives.

"Glad you could make it. There's some stuff going on that you might find interesting," Ken said. "This is still officially your case, isn't it?"

"Yeah," Droesch answered. "Until it's officially closed by the NTSB or the FBI as an accident and the final docket is published, we're still on it, and they tell me that's about a year from now."

Ken nodded. "See those two guys talking over there," he pointed towards Lopat and Shades. "One of them works from the NTSB and is here unofficially. The other is a retired airlines pilot who happens to be the first officer's father. Go over and speak with them, tell them I sent you over and just listen to what they have to say."

Droesch had known Staller since high school and trusted his instincts. The two detectives moved off and Staller moved towards Reaza, who was talking to an older man who looked familiar, but he could not quite place him.

He approached Reaza and the man she was speaking with and noticed that the reporter had taken a notebook and pen out of her pocketbook and was concentrating on writing down what he was telling her.

He didn't want to break her concentration and ruin what was obviously an interview, but he was both drawn to her and curious about what the man was telling her.

As he got close, Ken heard him say, "I got a really got a good look when the tarp was up, and the fuselage had lots of explosive damage on it. That was my profession for 30 years, and I know what I was looking at. I called the NTSB and told them what I saw and asked them to call me, but that was days ago, and nobody has responded until today. The woman who called told me that the fuselage had no explosive damage, that I must have been mistaken and that the crash was an accident caused by the First Officer overflying the rudder. That's bullshit, and it's time that people know the truth."

Ken wanted to hear more and he approached the pair.

Reaza heard him approaching and smiled at him.

"Ken, good to see you again," she said. Turning to the man, she said, "Jim DiGreggorio, this is Sgt. Ken Staller of the NYPD. He is not investigating the case, but he would be interested in hearing what you have to say."

"Jim volunteers at something called HARP," she said, checking her notes. "It's at Floyd Bennett Field and he had a good look at some of the wreckage as they were transporting it to the hanger there. He's retired Navy and knows about aircraft damage. He says there's explosive residue all over it that's clearly not from a crash."

Staller was not surprised, not after what he heard from Shades and what Reaza had told him of the informant in Brooklyn."

"Are you going to do his story," Staller asked Reaza.

"Can't, not my story. Aviation stories have to be done by Chuck Munat, the aviation beat reporter and he's at an airline-sponsored conference in Texas, fully paid by the airlines, I might add. I'm just here to take notes and give him any leads that come up," she said angrily. "Not that he'll want to do the story if it contradicts the NTSB report. He didn't even want to hear about Brooklyn."

"I have somebody who will listen to you," Ken said, leading DiGreggorio towards the back of the room, where Lopat, the two detectives and Shades were in a tight group, with the two civilians talking while the detectives listened. DiGreggorio will be a good addition to that group, Ken thought.

It was nearing 7:30 p.m. and the room was filled with locals, with a number of people still looking at tables, now filled with wreckage of various sorts, ranging from webbed seatbelts and harnesses to burnt and twisted metal.

In the corner, he spotted his son, speaking urgently with Lopat, Shades, the Newsday reporter, the detectives and a man he did not recognize.

He would give it ten minutes more and then start the meeting.

He noticed a young man and woman in the first row who were in an urgent conversation of their own. He wondered what the argument was about. The man kept glancing at him and then looking away, as if he had something to say but was not in any hurry to make his point.

Had he known that the man, Bobby Sallow, knew what happened to Flight 587 and had the proof in his pocket, he would have spoken to him prior to the meeting. He did not, however, nor did he know that Sallow was the man who called him after the crash to tell him that he had seen a missile fired from the bay his the plane.

Instead, when the discussion group in the back of the room broke up, Staller decided that it was time to start the meeting.

He moved behind the podium with the Beach Club's stylized logo, two seagulls outlined in blue over a looming beach and oceanfront.

He called for quiet.

"My name is Ron Staller and most of you know that I am the editor of the Beachcomber, the local newspaper," he said into the microphone. "I called this meeting because many of you who witnessed AA 587 in the air just prior to the crash, who witnessed the crash, or have found wreckage from the Airbus A300, have come to me with your own stories and I want you to tell those stories to this group tonight. "Perhaps you know that the NTSB and FBI have already declared this an accident – pilot error. There are many of you who know what they saw who dispute that. Perhaps after tonight's meeting we can come to some understanding of what really caused the plane to crash into our neighborhood. I just want to say that I invited the NTSB, the FBI and all of the daily newspaper's aviation writers, but none of them are here tonight because they consider all of you witnesses as unreliable, even though many of you are trained and experienced first responders – firefighters, police officers, EMTs."

He invited anybody who wanted to speak to form a line at the right side of the room. About a dozen people, including the man who had been speaking to the detectives at the back of the room, stood up and formed a line. As he watched the locals, most of whom he knew well, form the line, he noticed a man he had never seen before standing in the far corner in the rear of the room. The man pulled out a small camcorder and slipped what looked to be press credentials over his neck.

Staller noted that they were not the official NYPD credentials that he had to get each year. Both the man and the credentials looked suspicious, he thought. Maybe he was getting paranoid, but his only thought was that a federal agent, perhaps from the NTSB or the FBI was there filming the meeting to hear what they knew about the crash.

The first speaker took his place at a microphone that had been set up near the front of the room.

He was an older man, wearing an impeccable suit, tie and shoes. He seemed out of place because most of the others were dressed casually, in jeans and t-shirts or collar shirts.

He identified himself as Tyler Krebs, head buyer for Saks Department Store in Manhattan, and Ron could not think of what he might have to say. He obviously was not a Rockaway person, but perhaps he was visiting on the peninsula and saw something that day.

"I am here because I owe it to Carol Luczak," he said. Something in the back of Ron's mind recognized the name from the list of passengers who had died on the plane, a long list that he had printed in the last issue of the paper.

"Carol was one of my buyers, a crackerjack at her job and an up and coming employee. She was on the plane, flying to the Dominican Republic to speak with some of the better stores we supply clothing for on the island," Krebs continued. "Upon takeoff, she apparently remembered that she had something to tell me and called me on telephone in business class. She was talking to me when I heard a loud bang over the line and she told me that something had hit the plane from outside the fuselage and had exploded behind the wing. That was the last thing she said and she must have dropped the phone. I listened to the death throes of the passengers, and there was nothing I could do. I have been following the story in the New York Times and I saw nothing about an explosion, so I called the NTSB who put me on to the FBI. I told both groups the story, but they sounded disinterested and told me that they would note my call on the record. I was online and read about this meeting and felt obligated to come here and tell her story. Thank you."

As Krebs walked away from the microphone back to his seat, Ron noted that both Ed Lopat and the two detectives were moving to intercept him.

The next two people, a middle-aged man and woman walked up to the microphone. The introduced themselves as Broad Channel residents Timmy and Gerri Gregory.

They told of walking their dog south on Cross Bay Boulevard towards the bridge, something they did every day when the weather was good. Timmy spoke for the couple as his wife held his arm and closed her eyes, as if she were seeing the crash all over again in her head.

"We hear a roaring sound and something like a loud thud, and we looked up. There was a plane coming out of the airport and it was not going straight ahead, it was sliding sideways towards Rockaway," he said. "We could see dense black smoke coming from the other side of the plane, but we didn't see any flames. Then, the plane went into a flat spin, like a kid's top. For a moment, the nose of the plane came up and then first the tail and then the two engines, one after another, popped off. The tail fell into the bay near the water treatment dock and the engines went into the peninsula, but we weren't sure where. Finally, the plane spiraled down into the peninsula and we could hear emergency trucks and ambulances coming south on Cross Bay Boulevard as we watched. That's all we have, but we both definitely had the feeling that there had been some sort of explosion or fire on the fuselage."

They walked away, sobered by the remembrance of Nov. 12.

Rob Givens slipped into the back of the line. He obviously had something to say and had just decided to say it.

Another husband and wife walked to the microphone.

Before they could speak, however, Stan Shades got up from his chair and pulled an airplane model from his large briefcase, a large plastic model of an A300-600, the model of the Airbus plane that crashed into Rockaway.

"I thought to bring this because some of our witnesses might want to use it to show what they are describing," he said, walking up and presenting the model to Staller at the podium.

Staller gave it to the woman at the podium, who introduced herself as Kathy Royster and the man with her as her husband, Ken.

"Ken and I were in the diner for breakfast before going to work," she said, holding the model in her hand. "Rob was pouring a second cup of coffee for us when we heard a loud roar. Ken thought it was another Concorde, but there is only one each morning and it and it had already passed over the diner. "We all looked up and saw a regular airliner heading low right for the diner. We could see the side of the fuselage and it was on fire."

She held up the model and pointed it towards her head and showed the crowd where they had seen the fire, on the starboard side between the wind and the tail.

"Pieces of the plane, some small and some large, were falling off the plane. When it passed overhead, we could hear the pieces falling on the roof of the diner. It sounded like a heavy rainstorm. We ran outside and looked west and we saw a large plume of smoke and fire about a half-mile away, in Belle Harbor."

Royster gave the plane back to Staller and the couple went to sit down.

Another couple, with a teenage daughter in tow, were next up to the microphone.

Charlie Tanner walked over and took the model from Staller and went back to the microphone. He introduced his wife, Joan and their daughter, Jennifer.

"We were driving back to Rockaway after having breakfast in

Brooklyn that morning because we were all off for the holiday. We were just passing the entrance to the Belt Parkway and Jennifer was watching the planes leaving Kennedy. I had just got my pilot's license for single-engine planes and Jennifer was interested in getting one as well. In any case, I wasn't paying much attention, digging around to get change for the toll on the Marine Parkway Bridge, when my daughter yelled out that there was a plane on fire. I glanced over and saw flames on the starboard side, just aft of the wing. The plane slipped sideways toward the peninsula and then went into a flat spin. A plane that size doesn't come out of that kind of spin, and I realized it was going down. I pulled over to watch as we got onto the bridge and saw the tail come off. Then, more parts of the plane fell off and it augured into Rockaway. We saw lots of fire and smoke, and we called 911, but we could already hear sirens heading for the peninsula.

Staller saw that ex-firefighter Tommy Flynn was next in line. He and Flynn has discussed what he had seen that day and he thought it was a solid description. Tanner, walking away from the microphone, realized that he had not used the plane prop and he turned it over to Flynn.

Flynn was well-known in Rockaway and also well-respected.

Staller looked around to see if Lopat was still in the room and then noticed that the NTSB investigator was holding a small tape recorder, much like the one he used himself for interviews. Somehow, that was reassuring.

Flynn, who needed no introduction to most of the crowd, introduced himself and recounted that he had been jogging on the boardwalk when he heard a loud bang and looked towards the bay, sighting a plane on fire. He used the model to show where on the plane he had seen the smoke and flames. When he finished recounting what he had seen, he added, "I have been a fire officer for more than 20 years and have seen many, many fires and many other accidents and incidents. I know fire and smoke when I see it and I did not panic or somehow transform what I saw into a scene from a movie or television show, like the FBI and NTSB believe of eyewitnesses. That plane was on fire and it was losing both pieces and altitude by the minute even before the tail fell off."

A few other speakers came to the microphone, basically repeating what had already been reported. When the line ended, Staller said, "Now that the witnesses have told their stories, I know that a number of you have brought pieces of wreckage that you found near your homes in Belle Harbor. I would like you to come forward with that evidence and describe where you found it and how.

Several people go up and went to the two tables at the back of the room and retrieved what they has placed there. Then they got in line.

Staller started off the discussion by holding up the charred portion of a blue seatbelt that he had picked up in the street a few blocks east of the crash scene.

"This is a charred seatbelt that I picked up outside the crash scene," he said. "The color indicates that it was used on a passenger seat. It is charred and burned. That would have been understandable if it had been found inside the crash area. There is no reason, however, that it would be charred and outside the crash area if it had not been on fire while the plane was in the air, long before it crashed."

He did not mention the growing proof that the plane was shot down by a terrorist missile. He sat down next to DiGreggorio and Lopat.

Sarah Lefkowitz raised her hand from the audience. She held up a gray seatbelt.

She stood and spoke.

"I wasn't going to say anything, but I found this gray seatbelt west of the crash scene. I didn't think that was important, so can anybody tell me why the different color and what that means.

Lopat stood up. He did not identify himself as an NTSB officials.

"The blue seatbelts are used by passengers," he said. "The gray seatbelts are used by the cockpit crew and the flight attendants, who would have been in the rear of the plan during the takeoff." He walked over and took the seatbelt from Lefkowitz, turning it over in his hands, examining it closely.

He walked over and showed it to DiGreggorio. DiGreggorio looked at it and hesitated. Then, he stood up and addressed the crowd.

"I looked at the debris brought here tonight, and I had a good look at the wreckage at Floyd Bennett Field, even though the hanger where it is stored is guarded 24 hours a day by armed Federal agents," he said. "That begs the question of why, but I volunteer at the field and had a good chance to look at one load of the wreckage. I was in the Navy and helped investigate Green Board accidents – accidents where an investigation is ordered by the captain. The changes in the metal that I see tonight and that I saw on that truck, could only have been caused by a shock wave exerting immense but short-lived overpressure."

He looked at Staller.

"Could you put that in English," Staller said with a laugh.

"Something exploded here," he said and sat down, looking grim.

The audience, understanding the immensity of what DiGreggorio had just said, was stunned.

Staller stood up, as stunned by the statement as anybody else.

"I think that we have achieved what we wanted to achieve here tonight – a little truth," he said. "I would like to adjourn the meeting and ask a group of the principals, Mr. DiGreggorio, Mr. Lopat, the NYPD detectives, my son, Ken, Reaza, and anybody else who needs to be part of the group, to get together and discuss what we have discovered here tonight. Thank you all for coming. It's too bad that the FBI and the NTSB are not here tonight. It's even worse that the daily newspapers are too beholden to the aviation industry to even show up here tonight.

He looked up at the rear of the room and saw the suspicious man pack up his camcorder and quickly leave the room.

The audience began to get up and leave. Some of those who would be continuing the meeting stood around, waiting for the others to leave.

Lopat walked up to Staller, who was still standing at the podium, unsure whether or not he wanted to make himself part of the core group. He would have to write a story about the meeting, and he was not sure how he would do it without disrupting the real investigation into the crash.

Lopat shook hands with Staller.

"I'm at a crossroads here," he said sadly. "My boss has said that this is an accident caused by the first officer. We all know better. If I walk away now, I have some protection, but I'm going to have to tell them what went on here tonight. They will then disrupt the NYPD investigation and continue to cover this up. If I stay and meet with the others, I will be out of a job by tomorrow. No doubt there are some federal agents here tonight. It's a tough call, but I want to do the right thing. I'll meet with the others and then take the consequences. Perhaps it's time to move on in any case."

He walked away, joining the others, who had formed a circle of chairs in the middle of the floor.

Staller knew that he could not yet print all that he knew. He would be able to do that one day, but not tonight. He did not join the circle. Instead, he walked outside.

The fidgety man from the first row was standing there. The woman who was with him when he was inside was gone.

The man walked towards Staller.

Staller spoke first.

"It looked to me that you wanted to say something in there, but were reluctant to do so.," Staller said. "Do you want to speak in private?"

"Yes," the man responded. "First, I want to show you something."

He dug his smart phone from his pocket and tapped a couple of icons. He held the screen up and showed it to Staller.

At first, Staller did not understand what he was looking at. He could see the wall that separated Jamaica Bay from Beach Channel Drive. He was not sure what street the view was at. There was a small boat out on the bay, two men fishing.As he watched, the view expanded and he could see something with a large contrail rising into the air. The camera followed the object that was rising off the bay. The camera continued to rise and then a large airliner came into the scene – a large airliner with the distinctive Double A logo on the tail.

He then knew what he was looking at. A missile tracking AA 587. He suffered a chill, not from the night air, but from watching the passengers and crew on AA587 die in real time.

He watched as the missile continued to rise and all of a sudden it exploded behind the plane's wing. The plane began to spin and the tail fell off into the bay.

Staller was stunned. He had just seen proof that a missile had brought down AA 587 and that the government was covering it up.

He didn't know what to say.

The unknown man broke the silence.

"I want to explain why I cannot come forward, why my name can never be used, why I cannot testify," he said. "I am officially dead in the rubble of the World Trade Center. To come forward would destroy my life, cause my wife pain and change my world. I will not do that. I know that reporters must protect their sources. I expect you to do that for me."

Staller could only shake his head. He was not prepared for this.

His first thought was that he would show it to his son, who would know that the next legal step would be.

"Can I get a copy of that," he asked. "I promise to protect your anonymity, to never give up your identity, which I do not know anyway."

Bobby Sallow died in the World Trade Center," he said. "His name was memorialized and his wife is getting survivor's benefits. He no longer exists. I won't give you my new name, nor talk about my new life. I have been waiting for somebody else who saw the missile to come forward. Nobody has. So, I had to come here tonight and tell the truth. But, I will not allow Bobby Sallow to be resurrected."

Staller nodded his agreement. Staller asked Sallow to leave his phone and take a 20 or 30-minute walk and then meet him at Beach 116th Street and Rockaway Beach Boulevard, a block from the meeting room.

Sallow handed him the phone and walked away.

Staller walked in and moved towards the men and women in the circle. They stopped talking and stared at him.

"I have something to show you, but I can't tell you where I got it," he said.

The others looked at each other and then each nodded his or her assent.

They gathered around as Staller started the video. Nobody uttered a word until the video ended.

"Where did you get that," Lopat asked, sounding more like an NTSB official.

"I promised my source that I would not identify him, as is my right under the state's shield law," he said. "The man cannot be identified without changing his life and endangering his family. I can't provide his name.

"Is he breaking any law," Droesch asked.

"Not that I know of, but he might have," Staller answered.

Several of the participants asked to see the video again.

Staller replayed it.

"That's evidence of a mass homicide," Droesch said. "I need to take that phone into custody."

"Not until I speak with my informant, which will be in about seven minutes," Staller said, glancing at his watch.

Droesch clearly did not like it, but he agreed.

His son spoke up.

"I understand your reluctance to let us have the phone," he said. "But this is evidence of the murder of 365 people. It is evidence that the feds are covering up the fact that terrorists brought down the plane. Sooner or later, we have to either acquire the phone or the video with some sort of provenance of where it came from."

"Let me talk to my informant," Staller said, and walked away.

Sallow was waiting for him.

"I wasn't sure you would come back with my phone," he said. "Thanks for that."

"You might not have it for long," Staller said. "The cops want it as evidence of a homicide. I think they have a right to it and I think you do also. Otherwise, you never would have come forward tonight."

Sallow told Staller that he had already took everything else off the phone and was willing to give it to the police with the agreement that they would never know either his real name of his new name and that the police promise to never look for him in the future.

"I'm not sure they will make that deal," Staller answered, "but I will bring that to them."

"I want them to have the video, so you can give them the phone in any case," Sallow said. "If they won't make the deal, then I will do it if you promise to protect me as a source. I'll make it hard for the cops to find me."

Staller went back to the Beach Club. He explained the deal to Droesch and his son, but both shook their heads.

"We can't do that without going to our superiors," Ken said. In any case, I don't think the brass will agree to that."

Staller took the phone out of his pocket and gave it to Droesch.

"Take it. He wants you to have it. Don't ask me who he is, because I don't know, and I won't cooperate with you in finding him. I think he's doing the right thing," Staller said.

Droesch looked around at the men and woman gathered around him.

"I think that it is best for all of us if we keep this information from the feds," he said. "Something's going on and until we find out who is on our side, on the passenger's side, we can't let the feds know about this. They have a way of shutting things that they don't like down with a thud. We don't want to be under that thud when it hits."

The others nodded their assent.

Ron Staller nodded too, but this was a story that had to be told. He would tell it when the time was right. It was too early and too dangerous for him to run the story immediately.

He thought of Bobby Sallow, or whatever he called himself now. He hoped that Sallow was long gone and would never be found.

Reaza was stunned by what she had learned at the meeting. As a journalist, she knew in her bones that her duty was to return to Nassau County and the Newsday newsroom to write her story and turn it in to her editor for the first edition of tomorrow's paper. It would most likely make the front page.

Two weeks ago, she would have done just that. Today, there was more at stake – catching the terrorists, stopping another attack, harming the investigation. Then, there was Ken Staller. She stood by the door of the Beach Club, looking at the boardwalk and the Atlantic Ocean beyond. What to do?

Ken walked up to her. It was if he were reading her mind.

"Big Story, huh," he said. "Front page."

"Yes, front page. A career builder."

"What are you going to do?"

She hesitated. "There are so many unanswered questions. I'm not sure my editors want to challenge the government without some real proof, without a government official's comment. I could write it tomorrow, but it would never get published."

"So, you'll hold it for at least a while?"

"What are the chances of me staying inside, so that when the time comes, I will have information that no other reporter has?"

"As far as I'm concerned, you have been an incredible help in finding the terrorists. I have spoken about it with Billy and the others, and they agree that you can be a big help in ending this the right way. Are you in?"

She did not hesitate this time. It was a novice reporter's dream. Inside on one of the biggest stories of the year.

"I'm in."

The two touched hands and then her hand slipped into his as they walked up Beach 116th Street towards the parking lot, which bordered the boardwalk.

"Do you have to leave now," Ken asked.

"What do you have in mind," she asked with a twinkle in her eye.

"Some time together," he answered. "Come to my place for a while. For whatever happens."

She looked at him and smiled. She squeezed his hand.

"I would love to."

They walked in silence to their cars. She followed him back to his Beach 129th Street apartment where they both parked and, holding hands, walked into Ken's apartment.

XII

I t had been a week since the crash of American Airlines Flight 587 into the streets of Belle Harbor. The debris left by the crash had been removed, local streets reopened, bodies counted. Two hundred and eighty souls on the flight, five locals on the ground.

A memorial was held at Nearby Jacob Riis Park for all those who had died. The NTSB announced its preliminary findings that the fatal crash was an accident and that the final report would take a year or so to complete.

The yellow tape was removed, the crime scene was opened and locals began to go about their daily business.

The Beachcomber's most recent edition reported the final moments of the flight from the cockpit voice recorder. The front page headline was "What the Hell are We Into: Last Moments of Flight 587 Detailed on CVR Tape"

Neither the front page story nor the editorial pages mentioned the known facts – that the crash was clearly a terrorist attack on the United States by a group of terrorists with obvious ties to the Middle East and particularly the Saudi Arabian intelligence community.

All of the principal players involved with the investigation of the crash had been busy. Not the FBI, however. They were busy covering up the real cause of Flight 587, trying to shut down or impede the NYPD's investigation. Top FBI officials had gone to the city's Police Commissioner with orders to shut down the investigation based on

150

the fact that it had been declared an accident and therefore no investigation was necessary.

Both the police commissioner and the mayor, to whom the PC had bucked the decision, told the feds to take a hike, that it was their city and that the NYPD would do its due diligence on the case.

The investigation continued.

In fact, the demand by the feds to shut down the case piqued the interest of the high command at One Police Plaza.

Detectives Billy Droesch and Richie Cohen were called into the office of the Chief of Detectives.

Without speaking about the cell phone video, they read the brass in to the evidence they had already found – the connection with the marina and the abandoned rented car, the information from the Newsday reporter, the boat that disappeared and turned up in Howard Beach. The Muslim connection. The information that was developed at the newspaper's witness meeting.

"We have enough to go further," Droesch said, worried that the C of D's would shut them down. "In fact, we could use some extra help to follow the leads. There is a sergeant who works for the chief of the department who lives in Rockaway and knows what's going on. We could use him and perhaps two other teams."

"You've got them," the chief said, impressed with what the detectives had developed in such a short time. "Coordinate with my exec and he'll give you what you need, including all the overtime your secret little task force will need. Keep at it. The feds are going to learn a lesson that you don't screw with our investigations."

Four more detectives, two from the 100 Squad and two from the Queens Major Case Squad would soon get orders to reach out to Droesch. More importantly, Ken Staller would be detached from his citywide position and assigned to the investigative team as well.

Lots of things were already in motion and the new team members would held to sort it all out, interview witnesses and check out new leads.

For example, after reading the Beachcomber editorial last

Friday, he had realized that the man who made the video had contacted the editor right after the crash.

Based on the editorial and the information Droesch had developed, a judge granted a warrant to dump all of the papers phone call information on November 12 and 13, which would give him a list of all the phone calls to the paper on those two days – a key register that would list all of the incoming numbers – including those that were blocked by the caller.

In addition, they had put out the word to several precinct squads in Brooklyn that they were looking for a Muslim female named Zeata, who was involved with the Palestinian community on a confidential matter and that the investigation to find her had to be done "off the radar."

Just a day ago, the state had provided the name and address of the Muslim man who owned the boat that disappeared from the marina on the day of the crash and showed up in Howard Beach later the same day. The boat had already been confiscated by the cops and was getting a good going-over by forensic techs from the Crime Scene Unit, along with the abandoned rented automobile found at the marina.

All the activity had to be done on the "down-low" in fear that the feds would somehow mess up the investigation, perhaps seize the car and boat, take Zeata into and make her disappear, just like they did with the unidentified man who Tommy Lewis had killed while defending himself.

At the same time, specialists from the Technical Assistance Response Unit were working with the vital cell phone video, enhancing it and making several copies that would be safeguarded in separate locations should the feds barge in with a federal warrant and confiscate it.

———=»(((•)))«=———

Billy Droesch had asked Rob Givens to allow his ad hoc task

force to use a back room at the Beach Club as an office. Givens agreed and sealed off the room, giving Droesch the only key.

Notifications went out to the core investigative team for a meeting on Tuesday morning – Droesch, Cohen, Staller, Lopat, and the four new detectives: Doug Macleod, Tony Pinto, Tanya Grill and Brian O'Connell, all seasoned detectives with lots of experience in both Rockaway and with interrogating witnesses and perps alike.

He introduced them to Ed Lopat and explained his unofficial participation in the investigation.

Droesch used his notes to read the new detectives in on what had happened so far, detailing the evidence and where it had come from.

When he got to the cell phone video, he paused before talking about it.

"One of the most important pieces of evidence that this was a terrorist attack is a cell phone video taken by an unknown local," he started. "I don't know who shot it. It came from the editor of the Beachcomber. He got it from the witness, but he won't tell us who it is. For some reason, the guy can't come forward. I don't know why, but I have dumped the paper's phone records for the day of the crash and the day after, and we should be able to find out who he is. One of you will be working exclusively on that until we get the name."

"Needless to say, this information is only for the people in this room," he added. "Strictly confidential even to others in the department, and certainly to the feds who have already decided that his is an accident and are covering up the real facts."

He looked at Doug Macleod.

"Doug, that's your job," he said. "I'll fill you in after the meeting. Macleod nodded.

"I want you all to take a look at the video," he continued. "Most of you will be working on peripheral investigations, but I want you all familiar with it. It will motivate you to keep on track. It's frightening. Detective Elio Velez at TARU said we would have it later today, so we will convene at that time to take a look at it."

He handed out some more assignments.

Grill was to concentrate on the woman who rented the car and who spoke to the Newsday reporter.

Pinto was to concentrate on the Muslim man who owned the boat that was directly involved in the attack.

O'Connell, who had once worked in the Intelligence Bureau was to check out any chatter that the bureau had either before or after the attack, anything relating to November 12 and AA 587.

Staller was to concentrate on local issues and to see if he could get more from the Newsday reporter.

He and Cohen would meet regularly with the others and would coordinate the investigation.

Macleod spoke up.

"Why is this all on the down-low," he asked. "It's obvious that the feds are covering up the terrorist attack. Why?"

Staller fielded the question.

"We've been talking about that from the beginning," he said. "The only thing that makes sense is that they're covering for the aviation industry. How many people would fly if they realized that the plane they were on could be brought down at any time by a shoe-bomber or a terrorist with a hand-held missile? It's easier and more expedient to blame it on pilot error – one man, one mistake. Don't worry about flying. The aviation industry is a multi-billion deal with lots of lobbyists and with lots of bought politicians. Can't scare the customers. "

"I guess that makes a perverse sort of sense," Macleod said, shaking his head.

"Let's get to work," Droesch said, handing out files with all the information each detective would need. "We'll meet back here at 1800.

The team went to work. Ken Staller called Reaza Mahobir on her cell phone, figuring that she would be out in the field, covering some of the leads she had been developing on the story.As it turned out, she was in Brooklyn, trying to find Zeata.

She answered the phone on the second ring.

"Mahobir," she answered professionally. "How can I help you?"

"It's Ken," he answered. "I'd like to meet with you today sometime. Are you working on the 587 story?"

"I'm in Brooklyn looking for my source, who seems to have disappeared. She's not answering her phone and nobody here seems to know where she lives or even hangs out."

"I think the cops have people looking for her as well. They need to talk to her about her Middle Eastern friend."

"When can I write the story? I have enough now to create some doubt about the official determination by the NTSB and the FBI. That's a big story for me and could get me on the Metro Section news pages for good."

"I can't stop you from writing anything you want to, but publishing that now would create a lot of problems for the cops, who are trying to build a case against the terrorists and those who sent them. Even my dad is holding the story, and he has enough hard evidence to blow the feds out of the water. Can't you give it a little longer?"

Reaza hesitated. This was a big story. But she wanted to see the terrorists punished and wanted to see the feds explain why they called AA 587 an accident when they have all the evidence to prove that it was a terrorist attack. She knew that Ken would have to call the FBI and NTSB for comment on her story and that would alert them to the ongoing investigation and, perhaps, end it for good.

"Promise me your dad won't publish the story until I have a go on it as well. I don't care if we publish the same time, but my boss will be livid if a local weekly beats me on the story, she said.

Staller knew that he could not promise that his dad would do anything, but Reaza had given him the lead he needed and Ken was sure that his father would go along.

"OK, deal."

"Can we meet," he asked. He had more than one reason for seeing her again. He wanted information on the terrorists, but he also wanted to see her and perhaps find a way for them to get together again.

"I'm not getting anywhere here. Can you come to Brooklyn somewhere?

He knew a good Middle Eastern restaurant on Court Street in downtown Brooklyn that served a good lunch plate.

"How about the Eastern Star on Court Street," he said. "About 11:45."

"Fine, see you then."

She pushed the off button.

Staller got into his department car and headed for downtown Brooklyn.

———————————————

At the same time, Detective Tanya Grill, assigned to the 101 Squad, but working with the AA 587 task force was right around the corner from where Reaza was standing, trying to find Zeata as well.

She had called Reaza Mahobir earlier, but the reporter had told her that she could not help the detective, that the woman had asked to be kept anonymous and , like any reporter, she had to shield her source if that what she wanted. In addition, she had gone to the car rental office in downtown Brooklyn where the abandoned car used by the terrorists had been rented, but it had been a dead end. Both the driver's license provided by the woman who rented the car and the credit card she used turned out to be phony, which led the experienced detective to think that there were some big inter-national players behind the plot. Local scam artists seldom had to wherewithal to come up with such well-done phony identification and credit documents.

She had contacted the local Brooklyn precinct detective squad, which kept track of local Mosques and those members who es-poused the Palestinian cause as well as those who talked about radical Islam or who used social media to talk with others about the radicalization of locals.

They had searched their files and came up with three Palestinian women named Zeata. She had their last known addresses and was actively looking for them. She had found the first of the three on her list, but the woman had gone back to Syria two years ago.

She was working on the second, Zeata Mohammed, who lived above the stores on Court Street, across the street from the Department of Education headquarters.

She looked at the mailboxes inside the door of the six-story building and saw that Mohammed lived in apartment 5C.

She walked up the stairs, wondering if she should call for back-up from the local precinct. She decided to go it alone and see what developed.

She found 5C and knocked on the door. A television set played loudly in the apartment, tuned to a soap opera of some sort. She knocked again. "NYPD, I'd like to speak with you," she said loudly. "Just some routine questions."

Even with the television blaring, she heard a wooden window frame screech inside the apartment.

A runner, she thought. Maybe she should have called for back-up, some patrol guys to watch the rear window where there was most likely a fire escape.

She quickly ran down the stairs and around the corner. A woman wearing a head scarf was walking out of an adjacent alley. She confronted the woman.

"Zeata Mohammed? I need to ask you a few questions," she said.

The woman did not say a word, but tried to push past the detective as she pulled a small gun from her pocket.

"Get out of my way," the woman yelled. "You can't even talk to me. I know my rights. You're picking on me because I am Muslim. Get away or I will sue you."

Grill moved quickly, grabbed the woman's wrist and took the gun away. She pushed the Muslim woman down, flipped her and cuffed her. People began gathering on the street, yelling for Grill to leave her alone. Some started yelling "police brutality." Others took out cell phones and began shooting video of the takedown.

She pulled out her radio. "Central, this is Detective 51160. I need backup and a cage unit at Court crossing Atlantic, 10-85 forthwith,"

The central radio control acknowledged the 10-85 call, which meant that help was needed as soon as possible, one step down from 10-13, which means that an officer is in danger and needs immediate assistance.

She heard sirens in the distance and then two RMP's came screaming up Court Street the wrong way. The crowd began to disperse.

One of those on the edge of the crowd was Reaza Mahobir, who watched her informant get arrested. She was not sure what to do, but she would meet Ken for lunch in a little while, and he would know what to do.

The patrol cops broke up what was left of the angry crowd and helped take Zeata to the local precinct. Grill met them there, booked the prisoner and got an arrest number.

"She took the woman to her car, got on the radio and thanked the precinct officers for the backup and then headed back to the 100 Precinct, where Zeata would be questioned and then transported to Queens Central Booking for arraignment – unless she could get her to flip on the terrorist, in which case, she might well get a desk appearance ticket and a get out of jail free card.

―――●―――

Detective Doug Macleod was a long-time Rockaway resident, living in Rockaway Beach in one of the high-rise Mitchell-Lama buildings that lined Shore Front Parkway. While there was a restriction on working in the precinct in which he lived, he had worked in the neighboring 101 Precinct ever since he was appointed Detective Third Grade more than 12 years ago.

He disliked going to headquarters, to what cops called "1PP" or the "puzzle palace." Today, however, he had to talk to another detective, Elio Velez, who was one of the techs at TARU. Velez was one of the best computer techs the department had and he looked the part – beard, t-shirt, torn jeans. Not what one usually found at 1PP, but he was so good that he got away with it. Perhaps the fact that he seldom got into the field helped.

Macleod badged himself into the building and went to the fifth floor lab where Velez worked. He knocked on the door and let himself in.

Velez spun around on his chair.

"Hi, Doug," Velez said. "How are things in Rockaway?"

"Lots of action, thanks to the plane crash," McLeod said. "Do you have the enhanced video for me?"

"Yeah, quite a show. I understand that this is down-low and I can't tell anybody about it yet."

"Including the fee-bees, should they come around asking," McLeod reminded him.

"I can understand why."

"Could you clear it up any?"

"Sure. Didn't want to do too much. Don't want the feds to say I enhanced something that wasn't there in the first place."

McLeod laughed.

Velez handed him a package that held a few DVD's and the original cell phone in an evidence bag. Velez signed the custody tag attached to the bag. Macleod signed it as well. The chain of custody would be important if and when the case went to trial.

"Thanks for the good work," Macleod said, turning to walk away. He wanted to get the disks back to the Beach Club for the 1800 meeting.

———— ((●)) ————

Detective Tony Pinto had better luck than his colleagues. He had no trouble finding the Howard Beach man who owned the boat that was used in the attack. He had called the man, who claimed that he was surprised that the police had seized his boat and was unsure as to why they wanted it.

He wanted his boat back and he was willing to "go to the top" to get it, he told Pinto.

Pinto made an appointment to see him at his home at 11 a.m. and drove to Howard Beach, a predominately Italian neighborhood that once was the home and hangout of mob boss John Gotti and his family. He grabbed a quick breakfast at the Cross Bay Diner, a restaurant whose back room overlooked the docks that housed the NYPD's Harbor Adam launch. He drove to the Hamilton Beach section of Howard Beach and walked up the stone steps that led to the well-appointed home that backed on a canal that led to Jamaica Bay. He could see a walkway to a dock in the rear of the house, but could not see a boat docked there. Perhaps that was the slip for the boat that had been taken by the department.

He rang the doorbell. A middle-aged man opened the door.

Pinto flashed his tin and introduced himself. The man, whose name was Tamir al-Saudi asked him in.

"I have a few questions about your boat," Pinto said when they were seated in an ornate living room.

"Why did you take it? Nobody will tell me."

"We believe that it was used in the commission of a crime."

"How can that be? I left it at the dock when I went out of town on business and when I got back there was a note on my door that the police had taken the boat. Nobody used it and I was not even here for a week or so.

"When was that?"

"I left for Pittsburgh on November 3 and came back late on November 14. I had trouble getting home because JFK was closed after the plane crash."

"When was the last time you saw the boat."

"The day I left for the airport, about 10 in the morning on November 3."

"Do you have proof of your trip – plane tickets, hotel bills?"

"Sure, it was a business trip." He got up and went into another room and then came back with a sheath of papers. He handed them to Pinto. Pinto checked them. Made some notes in his note-book and handed them back.

"Everything looks okay," he said. "I'll have to check it out, but I have to tell you that somebody took your boat, perhaps without your knowledge, and used it for a major crime. We are checking it for forensic clues and then we may need to hold it as evidence. If not, then you'll get it back in a week or so."

He thanked the owner and left. He would check his alibi, but he was pretty sure it would check on. Not that the fact that he was out of town meant that he was not involved. It was a good cover story and he would have to break it down when the time came.

When he got back in his car, he called the Crime Scene Unit's garage in Long Island City, where the boat had been taken.

The cop who answered the phone identified himself as Nick Briano, the Lieutenant in charge of the facility, whom he had worked with him earlier in his career, when he was a patrol sergeant.

"We definitely have something for you, detective," the lieuten-ant said. "The report will be ready tomorrow morning, but I can tell you that there are some fingerprints on the throttle and the steer-ing wheel and there are burn marks that show some explosive in-volvement on the rear deck and gunwales that are consistent with the discharge from an explosive weapon,"

"Like a missile?"

"Exactly like a missile."

Punto told the Lieutenant he would come to Long Island City the following afternoon to pick up the report personally. Meanwhile, he reminded Briano that this was to be kept quiet, especially should the FBI come around asking questions. In no case was the FBI to get access to the boat without a federal warrant and, even in that case, he should be given a heads-up.

⟫⟪

Detective Brian O'Connell was sitting at a desk on the 12th floor at One Police Plaza, bantering with some of his NYPD friends from the time he was with the Joint Terrorist Task Force, the JTTF, which is made up of NYPD detectives, FBI agents, CIA whatever's and some retired cops and military types.

He was sitting across from Johnny Suskauer, his former partner, who had rotated back to his desk at headquarters after two years with the JTTF, a common occurrence in the intelligence business.

"What do you need Brian," his friend asked.

"I need to speak with you in confidence, somewhere away from here," he said lightly. "I need some information that the feds won't be able to track back to either of us. And, I need it quick and badly."

Without a word, Suskauer got up and threw on his jacket, leading O'Connell away from his cubical.

The two men went out of the building and walked towards Chinatown, only two blocks away. Neither said a word.

Suskauer led O'Connell into a small, crowded restaurant where most of the patrons were Asian, with a few tourists who thought the place looked realistic.

They ordered dim sum and some Chinese beer.

"What do you have," O'Connell asked.

O'Connell took a deep breath. He trusted Suskauer with his life. He knew that he would get no information from his old partner until he provided proof that he needed it.

"I'm working on a small, informal task force that was set up by the chief of detectives to look into the crash of AA 587 in Rockaway. We have solid evidence that the plane was brought down by a terrorist missile even though the feds say that it was an accident. I need to track some terrorists who came into the country in early November and then left for the Middle East right after the airports reopened a day or two later."

S uskauer paused.

"I wondered if the feds were covering something up," he said. "I can't believe that anybody would build a plane where the tail would fall off if the pilot overflew the rudder. It just did not make sense. What kind of evidence do you have?"

"Solid. A video that was shot by a bystander that shows the missile coming off the bay. The boat. An automobile rented by a Middle Eastern woman that was abandoned at the marina in Brooklyn that the boat sailed from. An informant who says that she hosted the terrorists in Brooklyn."

Suskauer smiled and held up his hand.

"Enough. I have heard about some Middle Eastern gentlemen who were in and out and who the Canadians say might just have come back to our fair soil. Let me check and I'll get back to you tomorrow. If there scumbags are back, then we have to assume they're here for a reason."

O'Connell thanked him and paid the check. The two men left and went their own ways.

————))((————

Staller met Reaza at the restaurant. She was already seated when he arrived and she did not look too happy to see him. He sat down across from her and touched her hand. She pulled it away from his touch.

"What's wrong? Did I do something to anger you," he asked.

I was close to finding Zeata when one of your cops came along, knocked her down and handcuffed her. Another police car took her away. I thought that we were cooperating on this and would have a chance to interview her again."

"Describe the cop."

Female, tall, strong, plain clothes. Dark hair, pretty, no makeup.

It was the perfect description of Tanya Grill.

"I know the cop. She works for the local precinct and was detailed to find her. I guess she did. She's good at her job. I can't understand why she knocked her down, though."

"She had a weapon."

"That explains it. She was protecting herself."

"It turned into a scene, with people taking cell phone videos and screaming about police brutality."

"Not good, going to have to develop a cover story when we meet tonight."

Reaza seemed less angry.

"What does this mean for me and my story?"

"This is coming to a head. We should be able to arrest her for aiding and abetting terrorism as well as a CPW charge."

"CPW?" She asked.

"Criminal Possession of a Weapon, he explained. "We'll have to hold the press off until we get the evidence to make the aiding and abetting charge."

They ordered and ate in silence.

"I would like to see you again," he said suddenly. "I know that you are angry, but this has to play out. There is too much at stake."

She agreed and smiled for the first time. She liked him and she wanted to remain on the inside. Losing her source to the police was a small price to pay.

The spent the rest of the meal making arrangements to meet that weekend. Then, the both had to get to work.

He kissed her lightly and she responded.

Then, they went their own ways.

XIII

W hile the police detectives sat in the back room of the Beach Club in Rockaway, Tafiq and Shafiq sat in the True Berger restaurant at Terminal Three of Toronto's Pearson Airport in Canada, eating hamburgers and cheese fries, waiting to check in and begin their flight back to JFK Airport, New York and hopefully the wide open arms of Zeata. She had been all he could think of since he was told by his new handler, Osama Bassnan, that they would be going right back to Brooklyn to bring down another plane, what he called a "one-two punch against Satan."

Osama has worked with Omar in Saudi intelligence and was involved with the 9/11 attack as well. On the record, he was an official with the Saudi Arabian Education Mission, which received all of its funds from the Saudi Ambassador in Washington, D.C.

With fraudulent, but perfect, Canadian passports provided by Osama, they should have no problem getting back into the United States.

They looked at the departure board outside the restaurant. Delta Flight 2837 would leave the runway at 10:30 a.m. and arrive at JFK less than two hours later. Then a cab ride to Brooklyn and Zeata.

They were told that they would be contacted the following day at Reaza's apartment by a representative of the education mission, who would provide them with a briefing and the weapons they would need to bring down another airliner. Osama would not go

---
165

into details, but it was clear that using a boat and missile to bring down the plane was not an option this time, that police patrols had been set and it was too dangerous to go that route again. Another method would be required, perhaps one that would finally bring them to paradise, Osama hinted.

They finished their food and walked out into the terminal. They had been smuggled into Turkey from Afghanistan and from there they used Turkish passports under bogus names to fly to Canada.

Getting from Turkey to Canada had been easy, a matter of greasing some police official's palm. Now, using the Canadian passports in their real names, they were on the final leg of their trip to New York City. They took out their passports and walked to the United States Customs and Border Protection Hall at the far end of the terminal.

They were told that they would not have to deal with a person at the customs hall, where automated kiosks were available for those who had Canadian passports and wanted to fly into the United States.

They stood in a short line and watched the procedure.

One by one, a traveler would approach the machine. They entered their name, date of birth and their passport number. A camera would take a photo that was apparently then verified by some sort of machine and a boarding pass was issued from a printer attached to the machine.

The two men were sure that their passports and photos would pass muster and that they would soon be back in America, ready for another mission.

Two Kiosks soon opened up and the men approached.

In a matter of minutes, each had his boarding pass and was heading for the gate.

By 10 a.m. they were seated in separate sections of the plane, waiting for the aircraft to push back and then take off for New York City.

When they arrived at Kennedy, they would be treated as domestic travelers, as if they were coming from another American city, because they had already cleared customs and would therefore not have to go through passport control at arrivals. A car would be awaiting them to take them to Brooklyn.

Both of them marveled at how easy it was to get in and out of the United States, even in the heightened security set up after September 11.

A nation that allows its people to move freely from place to place without strict restrictions and checks was always going to be vulnerable and there would always be somebody like them to exploit that weakness.

XIV

It had been a busy day for the cops working the AA 587 case, not only because they had a lot to check out, but because they had to do it quietly, without attracting the attention of the federal authorities who were also quietly working the case. While the cops were seeking to arrest those who killed 285 souls, the feds were working to cover up all evidence of anything beyond pilot error.

Luckily for the team, the FBI had no idea about the cell phone video, the female terrorist in Brooklyn, the boat and that were used by the terrorists in the attack, even though the car was found on federal property by Federal Park Police. To the feds, the case was just a stolen car, a domestic dispute that meant little to the bureaucracy that had not connected the car to a terrorist attack.

As far as the feds were concerned, that car found abandoned at the Gateway Marina was wanted for a simple domestic violence case. They didn't bother to track the owner any further, leaving that to the NYPD.

Droesch was sitting in the back room of the Beach Club, far from the prying eyes of the feds and from his own precinct.

He had made real progress that day. First thing in the morning, he had received the pen register for 718-634-4000, the telephone number for the Beachcomber. The register showed every telephone number that had called the newspaper on November 12, 13 and 14.

He quickly eliminated all the out-of-state numbers, knowing

that many media outlets had called the paper on the day of the crash and on the ensuing two days. Using the computer, he started getting the names and addresses for all the local numbers.

His intuition told him that the address he wanted was on the north side of Rockaway, somewhere near the bay, somewhere between Beach 108th Street and Beach 131st Street, where the crash occurred.

He had discarded two dozen probabilities when he came upon an address that fit the bill. 130-04 Beach Channel Drive. Worth a try.

He called his contact at the phone company and identified himself.

He provided the address and was told to wait on the line.

A minute later, the operator came back on the line.

"I have that for you sir, Toni Thomas, 130-04 Beach Channel Drive, Rockaway Park, New York, 11694."

Droesch thanked the operator and hung up. He knew in his heart that he had the right place and that he would find the man who shot the video at that address. Then, he would find out who he is and why he did not want to come forward.

That would wait until after the team meeting, however. He had learned to go to check out both witnesses and perps after eight p.m., when they were more likely to be home and finished with dinner.

————))(((())((——————

The other detectives started drifting in shortly after Droesch got off the phone. Within 15 minutes, the six men and one woman had formed a circle in the back room of the Beach Club.

They could hear restaurant customers moving in and out of the nearby bathrooms and occasionally they heard a toilet flush. Other than that, they were completely segregated from the diners and even had their own back entrance that emptied into an ally between the restaurant and the boardwalk, so they would not be seen coming and going.

Givens had set up a DVD player for them and a TV set so they could view the video when it came in from TARU.

Macleod was busy setting up the DVD player and the TV set was moved into a place in the circle, the others spreading out and making room.

Staller turned the lights out and Macleod hit the play button. The cops watched in fascination without saying a word as the enhanced video played. The missile had already lifted off from the boat when the video started, but the vessel could still be seen clearly. As the phone camera widened its view, they could clearly see a boat with two men aboard as well as the clearly-defined missile. As that missile rose, it was clear that it was a man-made and controlled device, changing course slightly as it rose. The phone followed its arc. As it got higher, they could see an American Airlines aircraft enter the picture.

As a group, they held their collective breath, as if they were willing the missile to miss the plane. They all knew too well, however, that it would not miss its target.

The missile and the plane were nearly touching when the proximity fuse in the missile blew up, tearing a petal hole in the rear of the fuselage. The plane began to spin and the tail fell off, quickly moving out of the frame.

Then, first one engine and then another popped off the plane as it augured in, nose first. Soon, it was out of the frame as well. The DVD ended.

Staller, who had seen the video before said, "Any comments, any questions, any doubt about what you're seeing on the video?"

Macleod, who had been in the Air Force for four years before his discharge, spoke first.

"No doubt. Unless you believe the conspiracy theories that say a man never landed on the moon, you have to believe that a missile shot down AA 587.

Ted Lopat, the NTSB's unofficial member of the team, wiped his forehead.

Those bastards in the FBI are going to hate you for this," he said. The NTSB is just obeying orders, but the FBI is driving this cover-up."

"They already hate us," Droesch said. "They think that we are all hayseeds with a subpar IQ and a remedial education, and that we all dress badly as well."

"What do we do with this now," Grill asked.

That was the question.

Staller had one answer.

"We bust the woman, the guy with the boat and the terrorists in the video and then we have a massive trial and use the video as evidence. Rule of law."

How are we going to do that," Pinto asked.

"We already got a start, Grill said. "I got Zeata Mohammad in a holding cell at the 100. Busted her in Brooklyn after she pulled a gun on me. We can hold her on the CPW charge until we can prove that she rented the car and gave aid to the murderers."

The others murmured their congratulations.

"Let's hear what the rest of you got out of today," Droesch, who was the lead detective, asked.

One by one, the others went around the circle, detailing their day and explaining what they had found and how they would follow up.

Staller spoke up after each of the detectives had their say.

"We have a problem. I spoke with Reaza Mahobir and she saw Grill make the arrest. There was a large crowd and some of them took cell phone videos. Reaza said that many in the crowd were chanting "police brutality." We're going to have trouble if some of those people go to the papers or to the television networks with the video. They're going to want to know who the cop was and why Grill made the arrest. When they find out she's assigned to a squad in Queens, that's going to raise questions as well."

"We'll have to cross that bridge when we come to it," Droesch said. "We can say she was working a Rockaway case and tracked a witness down to Brooklyn, but the woman pulled a gun on her, which is the truth."

They all nodded in assent.

O'Connell told the group that his ex-partner told him that there was a chance that the two men who shot down the plane were either in the city or coming to the city through Canada. He would find out more tomorrow.

They decided to call it a night.

"We'll interrogate Zeata tomorrow here at 0830," Droesch said. "Can you get somebody to transport her here under guard?"

Tanya said that she would take care of that and they all left by the rear door, looking like a group of diners who had just finished a late meal.

Droesch grabbed Sgt. Staller.

"We have one more job tonight and I need you with me," Droesch said. We have to go find the man who shot the video.

———— ((•)) ————

They got into Droesch's department car and drove north on Beach 116th Street and then made a left on Beach Channel Drive. They drove west to Beach 130th Street and parked on the corner. They found 130-04 Beach Channel Drive two houses off the corner.

Droesch knocked on the door.

A young woman answered the knock, peering out from behind the door that was secured with a safety chain.

"Yes, can I help you? Whatever you're selling, I don't want it."

Droesch showed her his shield.

"We need to speak with you and the man who is living here," he said, taking a chance that the man had called from her phone.'

Her face turned ashen.

"I live here alone," she said.

Droesch tried a white lie.

"A man has been spotted leaving here and returning each day. He is not in trouble, but we need to speak with him."

Toni hesitated.

"My boyfriend stays with me sometimes, but he doesn't live here."

"Can we come in?"

She opened the chain and stepped aside.

"Where is he," Staller asked.

"Watching television downstairs."

"Bring him up here," Droesch added. "Don't tell him who wants to see him. You're not in trouble now, but you could be."

Toni shook her head and walked down the stairs.

She came back two minutes later with Sallow in tow. He looked downtrodden because he understood that he had been found out. He wondered what it would mean for him and Toni, for his ex-wife who was really still his present wife.

"What's your name," Staller asked.

Bobby decided to give his real name.

"Bobby Sallow."

"Did you shoot the video that Ken Staller gave the police? By the way, Staller kept his promise to you. He didn't give you up. We dumped the Beachcomber's phone records."

"Yes."

"Why didn't you come forward? You broke no laws that I can think of.

Sallow explained and asked if there were a way that he could come forward and take credit for the video without losing his new identity and his wife losing all the benefits she got from the 9-11 charities.

Neither Droesch nor Staller could answer that question.

Droesch asked Sallow to come to the Beach Club the next day to give a statement that would validate his video. Sallow agreed.

The cops left, sure in the knowledge that they now had enough evidence against the terrorists should they ever be

XV

Sayed and Shafiq were comfortable but confused. They had returned to Brooklyn, to the apartment where they had lived with Zeata Mohammed before their last action against America. She was nowhere to be found, and there were mixed reports of where she had gone, some of the reports were troubling.

One neighbor had told the pair that Zeata has fought with a police officer and had been arrested for having a gun in front of the building. Two others told the same story.

A fourth, however, said that Zeata had packed up some of her belongings and left for a "vacation."

Shafiq was doubly unhappy. He was looking forward to climbing into Zeata's bed once again, with her beside him. It seemed that would never be. Too bad, but he had more important things to do.

Osama had come to the apartment that morning. He had brought orders and supplies.

Like Richard Reed before them, they were going to be shoe bombers. Or, rather, underwear bombers, he thought with a laugh.

Osama had brought them a Macy's shopping bag. Inside were two heavy pairs of white men's boxer shorts, but these were very special shorts. They were filled with a thin layer of plastic explosive, enough to blow a hole in thin aluminum skin of an airliner. In addition, there was a digital camera that had been rigged to act as the trigger for the two underwear bombs.

Also in the bag was an envelope with money and airline tickets

---

showing that they were booked on JetBlue Airlines Flight 405 from JFK Airport to Miami, Florida the following day, November 28th.

The tickets were made out in the names that were on their Canadian passports and similarly on their credit cards and Canadian driver's license. There would be no problem, however because they were flying domestically and already had their boarding passes printed out.

Osama outlined their mission, their last mission. They were both excited at the chance of striking another blow against the Great Satan and going to Paradise.

They were to sit in the window seats at the opposite side of the same row in the center of the aircraft. Their bombs would be set up simultaneously, causing rips in the skin of the plane on opposite sides of the cabin.

Osama said that the two tears would become a rip and the fuselage would rip apart, exacerbated by the speed of the plane and the air pressure as it climbed out of the airport.

The plane was set to take off at 8:30 a.m.

Hopefully, it would be in the Atlantic Ocean by 8:40. With a little bit of luck, perhaps they could drop the plane on Belle Harbor once again.

The money was to finance their last night on Earth, perhaps for some prostitutes or some other form of entertainment. Osama would not dare talk about alcohol, for it was forbidden to Muslims, but perhaps the money would be used for some of that as well.

———————(O)———————

While Osama was briefing the two bombers, two plainclothes detective from the NYPD's Intelligence Unit were sitting in a Con Edison van across the street, monitoring everything they said and did.

Elio Velez and other TARU cops had entered the apartment on a court order after Zeata's arrest and bugged each of the rooms. They had filmed the two terrorists when they entered and then Osama when he had showed up later on.

Johnny Suskauer, one of the detectives in the van, called Brian O'Connell.

"We got them," Suskauer said. "The same two that blew up AA 587 are back and plan to bring down a JBU flight out of JFK tomorrow. He gave O'Connell the names on the men's passports and the flight number. He proposed a joint action with O'Connell's team, his and the elite Emergency Service Unit.

He told O'Connell that they caught a bonus rat in their trap. They had run the picture of the man carrying the Macy's bag and Interpol identified him as a Saudi Arabian intelligence officer. He would not be arrested, but he would be followed and surveilled until they found out who his boss was.

As for our two underwear bombers, they would be arrested shortly after they entered the plane, before it even left the ground. We can't pack the plane with cops, because that could tip them off that something's up, but we have arranged to have the two outside seats next to each of them filled with cops, as well as the row in front of them and the row behind them. Most of those cops are intelligence or ESU, so that should give us and edge. Problem is, we don't know for sure what the trigger is. The shoe bomber had to actually take off his shoe and light it off. This is probably more advanced. Perhaps a cell phone or hand trigger. We'll have to move fast and hope for the best. Without the requisite airspeed and altitude, our experts say, the blast will have little impact on the plane that is still on the ground.

O'Connell said that he would alert his team to be ready to move the next morning. He would have a lot to tell the team when they met in an hour or so.

Ken Staller, Droesch, Cohen, Macleod and Pinto sat in a semi-circle in the back room of the Beach Club. In the center, facing them, was Zeata Mohammed, handcuffed to the chair.

"You can't do this to me," She said. "I didn't do anything wrong. I have rights."

"You mean, besides pulling a gun and assaulting a cop, aiding and abetting terrorism, accomplice to mass murder and whatever else we can add after you talk to us today," Pinto said angrily. She was obviously going to play the role of bad cop.

"Don't get so snippy," Droesch said to Pinto. "Give her a chance to say explain herself. Maybe she can help herself out and stay out of jail."

Droesch was the good cop.

"I didn't know she was a cop," Zeata said. "I thought she was trying to mug me."

Pinto laughed loudly.

"You piece of shit terrorist," she said to Zeata. "I identified myself at your apartment door. You chose to run rather than talk to me. Then, when I accosted you outside, you pulled a gun on me, was going to shoot me. I got you dead to rights and you're going to do some time in a state prison if you are lucky or life at Guantanamo Bay in Cuba if you're not, or if the feds get hold of you."

Zeata started to cry.

The comment about Guantanamo Bay apparently did the trick.

"They made me do it," she said suddenly. "I have family in Iraq. They said they would die if I did not help Shafiq and Sayed. I did not want them to die. What can I do to make it up, to help you?"

"Tell us everything and then write a statement that can be used in court detailing what you did and what you know of what they did," Droesch told her, handing her a yellow pad. "Start from the beginning with everybody's real name, fake name, age and where we can find them, Droesch said. "Do it right and we'll go to the prosecutor for you. We can make the gun charge go away, but the terrorist charge will be a little harder. The more you cooperate, the more that will go away. In addition, we also need the names and whereabouts of your outside handlers and contacts, along with their descriptions."

She began to speak, telling them all that she knew about the two terrorists and the handlers who had come to the apartment to meet with them. She identified a photo of Omar as one of the handlers, who disappeared one day. She did not know of his death at the hands of Tommy Lewis.

When she was through, they asked her some questions, asked her to make some clarifications to her written statement and then, after she signed and dated the statement and Droesch witnessed it, they took her back to the holding cell at the precinct.

They were talking about Reaza's confession when O'Connell walked into the room, accompanied by Detective Johnny Suskauer and his lieutenant, Nick Briano. The latter two had decided to help brief the Rockaway team for the takedown the next day.

Introductions were made all around and Briano asked to see the video. Macleod set it up and they all watched it again in silence.

"Jesus Christ," Briano said. "That certainly says it all and ties it up in a nice bow. What else you got."

We got the fingerprints of the two men on the boat that was used for the 587 attack. As soon as we bust the two skells, we'll know for sure. We got explosive residue on the boat from which the missile was fired. We have a statement from the Muslim woman who they lived with in Brooklyn, who also rented the car the used to get to the Gateway Marina. We have the tape. We have enough to take to court as soon as we find the two men. We also have the signed statement of the guy who shot the video and a statement from TARU that it has not been tampered with.

"We should have the two tomorrow," Briano said, surprising the Rockaway team. He explained and then briefed the team on the plans the JFK takedown on the following day.

"Each of the terrorists is in a window seat on either side of the cabin, I guess for maximum damage," he said. "Each will wear an underwear bomb, but we are not sure how it is triggered. That makes it important that we have our strongest people sitting next to them, cops that can make a strong takedown no matter what happens. Those cops will be hand-picked ESU cops, all of who have military special ops experience and the two nearest them speak Arabic."

Who will be in front and behind," Droesch asked, His voice revealing that he would like one of the slots.

"Since you developed all the information and have been involved from day one, two of you, probably Droesch and Pinto, acting as a couple, will be in the row behind the terrorist on the port side of the aircraft, ready to move if you're needed. One intelligence cop, probably Jonny here, will be with you. In front, we'll have three ESU cops.

On the starboard side, we'll have two ESU specialists next to them with Intelligence cops in front and ESU cops behind. They'll all look like tourists on their way to fun in the sun in Miami.

The rest of your team will be secondary, ready to go after the terrorists are neutralized to get everybody off the plane and secure the scene."

Droesch looked at Briano. "Is there any way Sergeant Staller can be on the plane? He was the one who brought us into this and his father who got us the video. His dad also hosted the meeting where we all realized that there is explosive residue on the debris."

Briano thought for a moment. He looked at Staller.

"Ok, he can take the place of one of the ESU people in the row in front of the terrorist on the starboard side. Any other requests?"

Doug Macleod raised his hand.

"Any way I can get on the plane? I've been waiting all my career for a bust like this one. "I'm a whiz with a camera, and can tape the takedown for later study."

Briano made a note to sit him in the row behind the terrorist on the starboard side.

"If that's it, we'll meet at 0600 at the FAA headquarters building just of the expressway," Briano said. See you then. Get some sleep and dress the part. Shorts, Hawaiian shirts, sneakers. No vests. That would be a tip-off."

He and Suskauer left.

There was a palpable excitement in the room.

It was all coming together and some of them would be in on the big show.

XVI

The cops who were set to board the aircraft to capture the two terrorists that Zeata called Shafiq and Sayed met in the back room of the Beach Club in Rockaway to make their final plans.

The aircraft in question was a Jet Blue A320 designated at Flight 452. It was due to leave JFK Airport at 8:30 a.m. bound for Miami, Florida.

Terrorist A, designated as Shafiq, although the cops had no way of knowing which was which at this point, was ticketed for row 11, seat A. His counterpart, designated at Sayed, was seated on the other side of the aircraft – row 11, seat F.

The cops had worked quietly with the airline to take over the six seats in row 10 and the six seats in row 12. Those seats would be filled with members of the Rockaway team, as well as specialists from the elite Emergency Services Unit. The two seats next to Safiq would be filled by ESUs officer Ken Yanek and Linda Adler, acting as a couple going on a Florida vacation. The two seats next to Sayed would be filled by ESU officer Doris Tare and Detective Doug Macleod doing the same.

Seated in row 10, in front of the two terrorists were Staller, ESU Officer Lynn Turbin, ESU Officer Vito Martino, ESU officer Sally Weber, Grill and Suskauer.

Seated in row 12, behind the two terrorists were Droesch, Pinto, ESU officer Ray Solga, ESU Officer Mark Tabor, Briano and O'Connell.

The plan called for the officers nearest the terrorists, assisted by both those in front and behind them, to be the prime actors.

Jet Blue executives cooperated with the NYPD, but wanted assurances that none of the other passengers on the plane would be harmed. The airline officials were asked not to notify anybody about the operation, including the FAA, telling them that there was a mole in that agency who might jeopardize the plan.

NYPD higher-ups, who brokered the deal, assured the airlines that this was the best way to take down the terrorists and still get a guilty verdict at a trial. They had to be on the plane and acting on their plan for the two terrorists to be convicted. The cops also explained to the airline officials that there was no way they could direct the other passengers off the plane without alerting them to the fact that something strange was going on, perhaps forcing their hands and an early detonation of the bombs. They had no choice to go with the NYPD plan, they were told.

The aircraft officials fearing that information that they refused to work with the cops to catch the terrorists would be a disaster for the airline. They acquiesced to the plan, with some misgivings.

The cops got ready to leave Rockaway for the airport. They would board in one and twos once the terrorists were boarded and seated. They had one main worry. They did not know how the devices would be triggered and they had no luck in finding Osama to ask him.

Experts at the NYPD Bomb Squad had some ideas, but no conclusive advice. The bombs could be detonated either manually, by setting it off with a primer fuse, or electronically, with a device in either man's pocket. In either case, the cops nearest the terrorists would have to be quick. The officers were also acting on the expert advice that should the devices be exploded while the plane was still on the ground, they would do little damage without the force multiplier of speed, wind and height.

In any case, at approximately 8:25 a.m. at a pre-arranged signal from a police official outside the plane, the pilot was to announce over the plane's loudspeaker system that "passenger Smith" was looking for a small, green carry-on bag, which would put all the cops into action and the take-down would be underway. A message that the passenger was looking for a small, red bag would cause them to wait for the "green" signal. That would also delay the departure and passengers would be told that there is a small mechanical glitch that had to be addressed. Experienced travelers would not think twice of a small delay in departure. That was a regular occurrence. Jet Blue Flight 452 would not leave the gate until the take-down was over.

———— ((●)) ————

The cops arrived together at Terminal 5, a terminal shared by Jet Blue, Hawaiian Airlines and a few local carriers. They entered the terminal in pairs and as individuals, all dressed as vacationers leaving for sunny climes with roll-on bags and heavy duty luggage, all of which was checked in just in case somebody was watching.

The cops all had weapons secreted in their clothing, small guns that could easily be disguised, thanks to the agreement with the airline and the security agency. With luck, they would all be off the plane with their two charges before the plane left the tarmac.

After the check in process, the cops all took seats in the departure lounge, glancing around to mark their colleagues and looking for the two terrorists. They had been given the surveillance photos from the Brooklyn apartment and had memorized their faces, even if they wore some sort of disguise.

At about 7:45 a.m. the two terrorists came into the departure lounge together, wearing cargo pants shorts and loud-print shirts worn loose over their belts.

Every cop in the lounge looked them over for clues as to how they would set the underwear bombs off when the time came.

The two chatted about how easy it was to get through the check-in and inspection process, laughing at the agents who had "scanned" them looking for weapons or explosives. Their special underwear had no problems passing muster and the plastic explosives inside did not even register on the scanning machines.

The cops were tense as they watched the two walk around the terminal, wishing they could take them right there and worried that they would blow the explosives in the hall, even though they knew that was not their plan.

The terrorists walked into the bathroom at the far end of the terminal, near the entry gates. Droesch told Yanek to follow them into the bathroom, see if they were doing something to prime the explosive, prod gently to see if he could get an idea of the trigger mechanism.

Yanek got up and sauntered into the Men's Room a minute after the terrorists.

A few minutes later, Shafiq and Sayed came out of the bathroom and walked to the Starbucks kiosk, each getting a small cup of coffee. The two then sat down in seats nearby Adler and Solga, both of whom had a smattering knowledge of Arabic. Droesch saw that as a lucky sign.

Yanek came out of the bathroom a minute later and sat down next to Droesch. Briano joined them.

They were far enough away from the terrorists and other passengers that they would not be heard over the announcements and general hum of the hall.

"Any clues," Droesch asked Yanek.

"Just a gut feeling, but I think they have a point and shoot camera rigged to explode their underwear. Push the shutter, and it goes boom. One of them was checking his camera's battery level when I walked in. Why check you battery level if you know you are not going to be around to see it run down?"

"Good thought," Briano said. "What pocket did he put it in after he checked it?"

"The cargo pocket on his right side," Yanek said thoughtfully. "Easy to access. That's got to be the drill."

"So we need to go for their right hands," Droesch said. "Easier on the port side of the aircraft than on the starboard, where that hand will be against the bulkhead."

The three men got up and started to quietly notify the other men and women scattered around the departure hall what they were up against and what they had to do when the "green" announcement was made.

It was a few minutes after eight when the gate attendant made her announcement about the flight.

"First call, Jet Blue Flight 452, Airbus A320 service to Miami, Florida, now boarding rows one through nine. Flight 452, rows 1 through 9."

About 40 people got up and shuffled to the gate. They showed their boarding passes to the attendant and walked to the skyway that would take them to the door of the waiting aircraft.

After a few minutes, the attendant got on the microphone again.

"Boarding Jet Blue Flight 452, rows 10 through 19," she said. "452, rows 10 through 19."

The cops waited until the two terrorists go up and walked towards the gate. They followed in loose echelon, trying not to look like they were together and on a mission.

The terrorists disappeared into the skyway.

One by one, the 16 cops followed the terrorists into the plane. When Yanek entered the cabin, Shafiq was pushing his carry-on into an overhead bin over his seat – row 11, seat 1. Just as Shafiq sat down, Yanek walked into the row and pushed his own bag into the bin. Then he turned and took Linda Adler's bag from her and placed it next to his.

"Which seat do you want, honey," Yanek said to Adler, knowing full well that she was going to sit in the aisle seat and he in the seat next to the terrorist.

Both Yanek and Adler were ex-military, he in the 82nd Airborne, she in the First Military Police Battalion, the elite group that investigated major crimes in the Army. They were friends as well as colleagues. Both of them were now in the elite Emergency Services Unit.

Adler settled into the aisle seat while Yanek sat down next to Shafiq.

He noted the fact that Staller was in the seat in front of Shafiq, ESU Detective Lynn Turbin next to him and ESU Detective Vito Martino in front of Adler.

Behind them, Droesch sat behind the terrorist, with Pinto and ESU Officer Ray Solga next to her.

Yanek nodded to Shafiq and smiled.

"Going to Florida for a vacation," he asked the terrorist.

"Business," he answered. "A couple of days."

Then Shafiq took a newspaper out of his cargo pocket, opened it and began to read, an obvious sign to his seatmate that he did not want to talk.

Yanek leaned back.

On the other side of the aircraft, ESU Detective Doris Tare was having more luck with Sayed, who seemed to her to be very nervous and happy to have somebody to speak with.

She and Macleod, who sat next to her came in separately, hoping that Sayed would talk with an attractive woman who seemed interested in him.

In reality, Tare was a tough ex-U.S. Marine who had been a drill sergeant before leaving the corps for the NYPD and had been one of the few women in the Recon Marine program. She had seen combat and she was well-trained in hand-to-hand both by the Marines and the NYPD. She looked to Sayed more like a young businesswoman on the way to meet friends for a quick vacation in the sunny south than a trained combat vet and an experienced street cop, which is just what she wanted.

As she chatted up Sayed, Macleod looked around, as if he were disinterested with what was going on to his right.

In the row in front of him were ESU Officer Sally Weber, Grill and Suskauer. Behind them were ESU Officer Mark Tabor, who was once an officer with the Israel Defense Forces, Lieutenant Briano and O'Connell, from the Intelligence Division, both of who spoke Arabic.

He noted that Tare was getting along well with Sayed, having already started a conversation with the nervous terrorist.

"How long are you going to be in Florida," she asked. "Maybe we can get together for a drink."

"Not long," he said, obviously wishing it would be longer. "I just have to do some business and then back to New York."

"Too bad. Couldn't you stay a day or two? It might be fun."

Sayed was unsure of what she meant by fun, but he knew he would like to find out. It was too bad that both of them would soon be dead, their bodies spread out over the ocean. He remained silent, not so sure he would be able to trigger the blast that would kill both of them and everybody else In the plane.

It was 8:20, ten minutes to takeoff.

The cops got mentally ready. The "green" call could come at any minute, certainly before 8:30.

XVI

28 November, 2001
0825 hours.

There were a lot of nervous people sitting on Jet Blue Flight 452 that morning. There was the normal nervousness of people flying for the first time, kids who squirmed in their seats with a few hours of inactivity and quiet on their parent's agenda. There were even two who knew that they would die on that flight that morning.

There were 18 passengers sitting in rows 10, 11 and 12 – 18 people all told, 16 of them who were cops dedicated to keep the plane safe and two terrorists, bound on bringing the flight down, just as they had to American Airlines Flight 587 16 days earlier.

Shafiq, sitting in row 11, seat A, next to the portside window and his colleague, Sayed, sitting in row 11, seat F, were both contemplating Paradise, with its verdant landscape and beautiful virgins. Shafiq was secure in the knowledge that he had control of the trigger and, with the flick of a finger, could bring it down at any time he wanted.

"Altitude and speed," he said to himself, repeating his handler's mantra. To get the maximum impact of the two underwear bombs that he and Sayed were wearing, the plane needed to be airborne at about 10,000 feet and climbing. He was told that the minimum time would be two or three minutes into the flight. Because the bombs had to go off simultaneously, the trigger he had in his right pocket would set off both bombs. Sayed had to do nothing but sit there and prepare himself for Paradise. It wall all up to him and that thought empowered him. He leaned back and relaxed, a smile on his face.

Ken Staller stood in front of the seat, fiddling with his carry-on in the overhead bin, looking for a book he knew was not there. He wanted to get a good look at his prey, Shafiq, who was seated in the row behind him.

He saw the smile on the terrorist's face and he wished that he could jump him now and be done with it. He had to wait for the signal that would trigger the take-down of both terrorists. They still did not know how the bombs would be triggered and whether one of both of the terrorists had the trigger.

⸺⸺◈⸺⸺

Shafiq looked at the people sitting next to him with some suspicion. He was always suspicious when he was on a mission. So far, that had kept him alive. Of course, it did not matter now. He would soon be dead and that thought was somehow reassuring. He did wish that he had more time with Zeata. He really had some feelings for her and he wondered again about what had happened to her. He hoped that she was happy or at least, at peace. He was not sure if there was a paradise for women like Zeata.

He fingered the small camera in his right-hand cargo pocket one more time to reassure himself that it was there.

The device was ingenious. The triggering mechanism for the bombs that both he and Sayed has layered into their underwear was inside a simple Canon point and shoot digital camera, except that pushing the shutter button would set off the two bombs rather than take a photo. It was so ingenious that the "camera" passed through the security check without a second look. He had worried that the security person would want to take a photo to see if it were genuine, but the woman just looked at it and put it back in the basket that held his keys and change.

It was right where it was supposed to be. Soon, he would use it to bring down another airliner, just as they did that American Airlines plane a few weeks previously.

Satisfied that it was there, he moved his hand back to his lap.

The move to his pocket and then back to his lap was not lost on either Ken Yanek, the ESU cops sitting next to him, nor to his partner, Linda Adler, who was sitting in row 11's port aisle seat. Both of the trained detectives decided that they would go for that pocket when the "go" message was broadcast.

————)((O)) ————

It was 8:28 a.m. and everybody was waiting. The cops seated in rows 10, 11 and 12 were waiting for the signal. The two terrorists in the window seats of row 11 were waiting for the plane to push back and then take off. A few minutes after the takeoff on Runway 35L and it would be over.

The captain's voice came over the loudspeaker.

"This is Captain Tom Tobin," the voice said. "Welcome to Airbus service to Miami, Florida. The temperature today is Miami is a sunny 82 and our flight will last a little under three hours. Please fasten your seatbelts for takeoff."

He clicked off. The plane did not move.

The cops picked up the sound of an NYPD helicopter overhead, hovering over the cockpit to make sure that the plane did not take off. Staller hoped that the terrorists would not hear the copter and blow the bomb prematurely.

The cops tensed. It was almost time to go. One way or another, a coded message would be transmitted in the next few minutes. Green for go, red for hold.

The click of the intercom coming on could be heard throughout the cabin.

"Passenger Smith is looking for a small green carry-on bag," the voice said. "If anybody sees it, please report it to a cabin attendant."

On either side of the plane there was a blur of action as the cops began to execute the plan.

Ken Yanek leaned over as if he were going to say something to

Shafiq. Instead, he grabbed his right arm in a tight grip, pulling it upward and away from the terrorist's pocket – away from where he was sure the detonator was sitting.

At the same time, both Ken Staller and Bobby Droesch reached over their seats, grabbing the terrorist's hands and pinning him against the seat.

The same scene was replicated on the starboard side of the plane, where Doris Tare grabbed Sayed's hand to keep it away from his pocket, while at the same time, Suskauer and O'Connell reached over their seat to pin the terrorist to his seat, immobilizing him the seat.

The cops on the aisle began their plan to move the other passengers on the plane towards the exits, which had been opened and ready for use by the ground crews and the flight attendants. They wanted everybody off the plane as quickly as possible and the slides deployed as the frightened passengers moved quickly to the exits, unsure of what was happening and nervous so soon after 9/11.

Sayed, who did not have a trigger, allowed himself to be overwhelmed and surrendered to the cops. There was nothing he could do. It was all up to Tafiq to blow up both of their bombs, hoping he would succeed and kill not only the cops that surrounded him, but the two of them as well. They had failed. Without being airborne, the bomb would cause some damage, kill those closest to the blast, but would not fulfill their mission.

Shafiq also realized that the mission was a failure, but still wanted to go out in a blaze of glory, to achieve Paradise and he could do that by at least destroying the plane and the tormentors who were all over him.

How they found him did not matter. He had to blow the bombs.

He threw an elbow at the man sitting next to him, catching him in the throat, freeing his hands for a second. He reached to his cargo pocket. He had to get to the camera detonator.

Ken Staller saw what was happening. He jumped over the seatback and landed sideways in Tafiq's lap. He grabbed for the man's right hand and succeeded in forcing it away from the pocket. Droesch still had a grip on the terrorist's left hand.

He awkwardly punched Tafiq in the face, bloodying his nose and forcing his head back into the seatback. Staller knew that the man could not get to the detonator that he apparently had in his right pocket somewhere or they might all die. He was glad, however, that they had kept the terrorists at bay long enough to get the other passengers off the plane. He hoped that Tare, Suskauer and O'Connell were more successful on the other side of the plane.

He threw another punch at the terrorist, but without much leverage, he could not put much power behind it.

"Open his seatbelt," Droesch yelled. Staller reached under his body and released the terrorist's seatbelt.

Droesch and Pinto pulled the terrorist up, not an easy job with Staller on his lap. They pulled his body up and away from his seat, each grabbing his wrist and pulling violently upward. They did not care that they might break his arm of his wrist. They needed to get to that pocket and liberate the detonator.

Tafiq fought back as much as he could, but with three or four men surrounding him and punching him, grabbing him, there was not much he could do. He tried to push his right side against the seat, hoping that would push the camera's shutter release, setting off the bombs.

It was his last chance. Now, however, his body was being lifted away from his seat, from the bulkhead. He struggled to free his hands, but he could not.

They pinned him to the top of the seatback. He felt hands probing him, reaching into his pockets, first his regular pocket, which was empty and then into the cargo pocket, where the vital detonator sat.

Staller felt the camera, knew right away that it was a point and shoot.

"I think I got it," he yelled to nobody in particular. "Hold him tighter. I'm going to get this to the bomb squad outside." Staller slid down the escape chute right into the hands of the NYPD's bomb squad, detective clad in heavy armored suits.

"I'm sure that this is the detonator," he said to the science fiction character in front of him. "We'll deliver the two man and their bombed-up underwear in a few minutes."

"Treat him gently," the bomb tech responded. "Take the two perps to the bomb truck over there and we'll defuse their underwear." He pointed to one of two large armored trucks standing nearby. "Be careful. We don't know how fragile the plastic explosive is until we test it and set it off."

Staller turned and ran up the rolling staircase that had been placed by the open front door that went into the plan just aft of the cockpit.

When he got into the plane, he saw that Suskauer and Droesch had handcuffed the two cursing terrorists. One of them was thrashing violently, apparently trying to set the bomb off by impact. It was not working.

"Get those two out to the bomb disposal trucks outside the plane," Staller said. "They're ready to strip them of their underwear and take it to Rodman's neck," referring to the NYPD's shooting range and bomb disposal facility in the Bronx.

They pulled the two to their feet and dragged them off the plane. The terrorists were soon in the vans, with detectives in bomb disposal dress removing their clothing and replacing it with green jumpsuits.

They would be transported to the lockup at the 100 Precinct, about 20 minutes away, while their clothing would wind up in the Bronx, along with the detonator, now disarmed and tucked neatly in an evidence bag.

"How come you're going to take them to the 100 rather than central booking or One PP," Staller asked.

"We're going to treat this as a mass murder of 265 souls within the confines of the Borough of Queens," Droesch said. "We have to do this by the book because murder is a state matter while terrorism is a federal crime. The feds are going to be all over this and if we let them take it away from us, we're liable never to see these mopes again and the feds will tell the papers that they never existed."

Staller shook his head.

The two terrorists came out of the vans wearing green NYPD jumpsuits with flack vests over them. They were led to separate 100 Precinct patrol cars and driven away.

At a neighboring gate, Staller saw the passengers from the flight being led over the tarmac to another plane that would take them to Florida. Many of them glanced over to their original flight, wondering what they had just seen.

The terrorists would eventually be transported to Queens Central Booking in Kew Gardens, just a few exits north of the airport on the van Wyck Expressway and arraigned by an assistant DA on 265 counts of first degree murder.

In any case, the clear and present danger was over and dozens of detectives were out searching for Osama to bring him

XVIII

The detectives and officers who had made the arrest on Jet Blue 452 the day previously stood strung out behind top police brass and FBI officials at One Police Plaza as dozens of TV cameras hummed, digital cameras whirred and print reporters took notes in narrow notebooks. It seemed as if every official in the city wanted a piece of the story that was front page in every one of the daily newspapers.

"Muslim Shitty Pants Bombers Busted," said the front page of the New York Post

"Arab Pants Fail to Blow, Cops Save Hundreds," said the front page of the New York Daily News.

"Several Long Islanders Saved as Cops Stop Terrorist Bombers," said the front page of Newsday, the Long Island newspaper.

"Alleged Middle Eastern Underwear Bombers Arrested in JFK Incident," the venerable New York Times reported on its front page.

The Mayor had just finished speaking, stating how proud he was of his police commissioner and the police officers who broke the plot and arrested the bombers before they could do any damage.

Then he introduced the FBI Agent-in-Charge, who began by congratulating the New York City Police Department and his own agents who, he said, "had worked closely with the local police every step of the way."

"What a crock of shit," Ken Staller said to himself. He looked at

Billy Droesch, standing next in line and could tell that he was thinking the same thing.

The FBI had no involvement with breaking the plot, finding the terrorists or arresting them before they could bring down the airliner.

"These two terrorists, who were sent here to bring down an airliner on American soil, will be prosecuted to fullest extent of the law," the FBI AIC said. "We have transferred the two to federal custody and they will be tried for their terrorist activity in attempting to bring down the airliner yesterday."

Staller had a sick feeling in his stomach.

"What about American Airlines 587," he thought. "Why didn't he mention their involvement with bringing down that plane just a few short months ago?"

He and Droesch looked at each other and it became clear to both of them immediately that the government was going to maintain the fiction that the crash of AA 587 was due to pilot error. They were going to cover up the fact that the same two terrorists killed the 385 people who died in that incident.

The AIC finished his speech and turned the microphone over to the city's Police Commissioner, who praised his detectives, his chief of detectives, his first deputy, the mayor and the FBI.

Again, no mention of the previous terrorist attack.

No mention of the evidence against the two terrorists. No mention of how they were tracked through the previous terrorist attack. No mention of the tape showing a missile bringing down AA 587.

The speeches ended and the questions began.

Reaza Mohamad raised her hand and was recognized, probably because of the head scarf she was wearing as much as for her journalistic chops.

This question is for the police commissioner," she said. "How did your detectives get on the trail of the two terrorists? Were they involved in previous actions, or was there an informer involved in the process?"

The commissioner stepped to the microphone.

"The detectives involved have been watching the two men for some time," he said. While they were never involved in overt activities in this city previously, their contacts and their activities made the detectives suspicious and they managed to get an undercover agent into the small cell. That undercover detective, who will remain anonymous still he is still involved in his undercover work, broke the case and led to the arrest. It was just good old-fashioned police work."

Reaza looks startled by the answer.

"A follow-up, please commissioner," she yelled a little too loudly. "There have been rumors that the two were involved in a previous incident at the airport. Can you confirm or deny that information?"

"The FBI AIC spoke up over the voice of the commissioner, who had started to answer the follow-up.

"Lots of reporters have questions, Miss Mohamed," the AIC said loudly. "I'm afraid we'll have no time for follow-up questions."

The press conference went on and Reaza sat down with a solemn look on her face. She glanced at Ken Staller on the stage and caught his eye. He looked both angry and determined. So did Bobby Droesch and the other detectives in the rear of the stage.

Staller was determined.

"This is not going to end here," he thought to himself. "We can't let them cover up the AA 587 mass murder. We owe the truth to the passengers and crew, to the people who died on the ground, and to the first officer who was blamed for causing the crash by overflying the rudder."

A New York Times reporter stood.

"I'd like to renew the questions asked by the Newsday reporter," he said. "Talk from some confidential informants says that the two terrorists who were arrested were somehow involved with the crash of American Airlines Flight 587 as well. Could you comment on that?"

The FBI AIC took the microphone. "There is absolutely no truth to that," he said. "No evidence that they or any other terrorists were involved. The NTSB has issued a preliminary report that says it was pilot error and we have found no evidence to refute that. Case closed."

The police commissioner remained silent, looking pained, but he was determined never to say the words "pilot error" when he knew that was an outright lie.

Both Staller and Droesch wanted to do something, to shout out the lie, to walk off the stage, but either would have ended their careers, they knew.

They stood silently until the press conference ended. As everybody walked off the stage and the top cops were all gone with their details and bodyguards, Staller grabbed Droesch, Macleod and Cohen.

"We have to talk," he said.

"About what," Droesch answered.

"You know what. We can't let AA 587 end like that, with all we did and with all we can prove."

"What can we do?"

"Got to think this out. Got to do something. The feds are out of the picture. We have to prove a cover-up that the feds have orchestrated and that One PP is obviously going along with, so our only hope is the Queens DA, who can bring murder charges of his own against them."

Droesch looked skeptical, but shook his head.

"Let's go for it," he said. "Almost time to get my pension anyway."

—«(●)»—

Queens District Attorney Andrew Bathgate had held the office for decades. His staff called him "Judge," because he had been a criminal court judge before running for the office and was highly-respected as both a keen political animal and as a no-nonsense prosecutor. It had been years since anybody dared to run against him for the seat and he most-often got the endorsements of both major parties.

Although he often had to work with federal prosecutors and the FBI, he always housed a resentment when they came into his jurisdiction to take over a case that might have federal overtones.

He thought of that once again as he faced three very angry NYPD cops who were pitching him an unbelievable tale about a mass murder that was being covered up by those same federal prosecutors.

They were also pitching him a case that might well end his political career if it were not true, or at least if he could not prove it to a jury.

The district attorney knew detective Billy Droesch well. His father had been one of Brown's investigators early in his career. Droesch had always been solid in the cases he brought to the DA's office. That was the only reason that Bathgate agreed to meet the three cops, to go outside the official chain of command. He knew that the three men were putting their careers on the line by coming to him off the grid.

Bathgate looked at the three men across his desk -- Droesch, a levelheaded, experienced detective; his partner, Richie Cohen, a younger detective who Brown did not know well and Ken Staller, a sergeant with a citywide planning and training unit, whose father was a local newspaper editor. Bathgate knew his father well, because the paper had recently endorsed him and he worked closely with the DA's press people.

Droesch could see that Brown was hesitant, even after he had laid out the evidence they had developed. He was holding the video for last, a kind of closer.

"Judge Bathgate, I want to thank you for seeing us on this, but there are two men waiting outside the building who you really should talk to before you make a decision," he said. "They could be here in five minutes, if you want some corroboration. One of them is an investigator for the NTSB who knows that really happened to AA 587. The other is Sergeant Staller's dad, a newspaper man who has seen the evidence and has held up from printing the story so that the two men who shot down the plan can be brought to justice. Would you see them?"

Bathgate had the sense that this was the last official chance the cops had to prove their case. He knew, however that their story would not end with him, that it would go public no matter what he decided to do. If they were right, he had to move the case ahead, even if it was political dynamite to buck the feds and the airlines on such an important issue.

"Bring them up," he said, reaching for his office phone to tell his security to pass the two men through. They waited without speaking until Bathgate's phone rang less than five minutes later. The elder staller and Ed Lopat had been waiting in their car on Queens Boulevard for the summons.

The two men walked into the room. Staller carried a laptop computer. Introductions were made.

Bathgate spoke first.

"Mr. Lopat, I know you are an experienced investigator with the NTSB, an agency who has said publically that his was an accident. Why are you here telling me that it was a terrorist attack – if that is what you are here to tell me?"

"That is what I am here to tell you, Judge," Lopat said quietly. "I have seen the compelling, irrefutable evidence that the plane was brought down by a missile shot from Jamaica Bay by the two men who were recently arrested for trying to bring down the Jet Blue flight. I am convinced the evidence if real and that my agency is covering up the terrorist attack because the truth would probably put a big hole in the number of people who would voluntarily get onto an airliner for a long time."

He looked intently at the DA.

"This will mean my career with NTSB is over," he added. "But it's the right thing to do. People have the right to know what really happened to those people. I believe that you have the right to bring murder charges against the two men, which takes precedence over the federal attempted murder and terrorism charges – sir."

Rob Staller spoke up.

"Judge, I have one last piece of evidence you need to see. We have been holding it for last. This came to me from an anonymous source who will come forward at trial if necessary. We all believe it to be genuine and I have had experts test it for its authenticity and it passed every test. We have a chain of evidence that puts the two terrorists in New York City, on a boat in Jamaica Bay on the day American Airlines Flight 587 was shot down. Now, we have the evidence that the jetliner was indeed shot down."

He opened the laptop, clicked a few keys and turned the screen towards Bathgate. The men did not need to see the video. They had each seen it numerous times since Bobby Sallow had turned it over to Staller.

Bathgate watched the video and then asked for it to be played again.

He watched it three times before asking that it be turned off.

"Are you sure that's authentic?" he asked. "I'm going to need to speak to the person who shot that video."

Ron Staller explained the problem and the reason that the person who shot the video was reluctant to come forward.

Bathgate laughed.

"We have had a couple of cases of "dead" people who were supposed to have been in the World Trade Center have shown up very alive," he said. "I still have to speak with him, but I'll try to keep him from testifying if it comes down to that. Hopefully, after I bring the charges, the feds will realized the error of their ways and will add the AA 587 charges to the Jet Blue charges."

"Then you will bring the charges," Droesch asked.

"Get me all of your evidence and let my investigators take a look," the DA said. "I should have an answer in a day or two, but I am sure that we will take this to a Grand Jury later this week."

Droesch pulled a large accordion file from under his chair. It included copies of everything they had connecting the two terrorists to the AA 587 attack. He handed it over to the district attorney with a solemn nod.

Bathgate took the packet and placed it on the corner of his desk.

The five men got up, shook hands with the district attorney and walked out together.

"That cut it," Lopat said. "The end of an era, and I'm not sure for what."

"What do you mean," Ron Staller asked.

"Even if he gets the grand jury to indict them, do you really think the feds are going to allow them to go to trial?"

"They have to, they'll have no choice because public opinion will force them to allow a trial. People will really be angry," the elder Staller said angrily.

Lopat scoffed. "You don't know the FBI and the NTSB like I do. They'll try and discredit our evidence. They won't go down easily."

"We did the right thing," Droesch said. "Now, it's out of our hands. Bathgate seems interested, even excited in bringing the charges, if only to screw with the feds."

"I'd like to be the fly on the wall when Brown talks this over with his investigators and his political advisors," Ken Staller said. "After all, the bottom line is that he is a politician, and you never can tell what might be in his political interest."

The men exited the building and walked to their cars,

Bathgate did not wait long to bring in his closest advisors, both prosecutorial and political.

He outlined the case that had been made by the cops and the evidence that they had brought to his attention. The recitation took nearly an hour, but not a word was said by Bathgate's subordinates.

Finally, he showed them the video showing the missile streaking out of a boat on Jamaica Bay.

"Recommendations," he said as the video ended.

As expected, Judy Gerritas, Bathgate's chief trail assistant spoke first.

"We have detailed evidence that the two perps murdered 265 souls within the jurisdiction of Queens County," she said. "I don't see that we have any choice but to take this to the grand jury, to arraignment and then to trial."

Ron Greshner, the DA's top political advisor chimed in.

"There is no way that this is going to be kept on the down-low," he argued. "Can you imagine the political fallout that will come when it breaks in the New York Post? We might as well all move to Nebraska right now and save some trouble. Your constituents – the voters – expect you to prosecute and perhaps the feds won't let you, but you have to go through the process and let the feds try and stop you. That will make you the hero of the piece. There is no political downside to going to the grand jury and indicting them."

Bathgate nodded.

Anybody else?

Bathgate's chief investigator, Donny Moran, a former first grade detective with the NYPD was looking through the evidence folder.

"I know Droesch and he's solid," Moran said. "I want some time to look through the evidence he gave you, but a quick read shows that this is a good case. They have the two perps in the area, they have them discussing the crime, and they have the rental car and the boat. They have all the connections. If we can get the NYPD divers in the water, we have a good chance of finding the discarded missile launcher. And, we have the video, even though we really need the person who shot the clip to come forward. I'm afraid the newspaper guy is going to have to give him up. That clip is the key. I say we go and we go hard and fast. We can't let the feds cover up 265 murders, even to save the airline industry a couple of million bucks."

Bathgate went around the large table, and the consensus was for moving the case forward.

"Do we have a sitting grand jury," he asked his administrative assistant.

"Yes," she answered. "They'll in teed up tomorrow morning at 9 a.m."

He turned to Gerritas.

"Will you be ready to present by then?"

"It's been some time since I pulled an all-nighter, but we'll be ready to present. Those folks are in for a treat tomorrow morning after hearing all those drug and robbery cases. Two hundred and sixty-five homicides. The second most-deadly aircraft upset in American history. We'll be ready."

Bathgate nodded.

"Let's get to work. I have some telephone calls to make," he said. "We're going to seriously piss off some justice department types, but that's the way it goes."

The staff filtered out as the DA turned to his phone.

——————)((•))(——————

Jim Morrison was the Agent-in-Charge, the AIC of one of the largest and busiest FBI offices in the nation. He was in a meeting with one of the justice department's prosecutors on the terrorist case when his executive assistant knocked on the door and stuck his head into the large corner office in downtown Manhattan, close to the Brooklyn Bridge.

"Judge Bathgate on line one," the assistant said. "Says it's important and imperative."

Morrison sighed. Bathgate was often a pain in the ass. For two reasons. His agenda often was not that of the federal government and he was a tenacious political operative. He wondered what he wanted this time.

He motioned the justice department lawyer out of the office and then picked up the phone.

"Judge Bathgate, what can I do for you on this fine day," Morrison said.

"I think I'm about to ruin your fine day," the DA answered with a chuckle. "My grand jury is about to arraign your two terrorists on 265 counts of felony murder and possession of terroristic weapons. In a few minutes, you'll be served with a warrant asking you to produce the men and turn them over to NYPD detectives for incarceration in the Tombs until we can bring them to trial."

"What murders are you talking about, Judge," Morrison asked, confused. "They were arrested prior to carrying out their attack."

"Not the Jet Blue airliner, the crash of American Airlines Flight 587 in Rockaway on November 12."

"That was an accident, Judge. The NTSB says so and so do we. They two men had nothing to do with that crash."

"We have overwhelming evidence that the two men you hold for the Jet Blue plot actually shot down 587 with a missile from a boat in Jamaica Bay. Overwhelming evidence, including a video of the actual missile shot."

"Can't be. Do you know what kind of trouble a prosecution like that would cause the airline industry, including all that business in Queens at JFK and LaGuardia? Perhaps you should rethink your prosecution before you get your office into trouble with the Department of Justice."

"Are you threatening me, Jim?"

"Not at all, just pointing out that everything we have says that 587 was an accident. In fact, there was no explosive residue on the aircraft. The facts are on our side in this."

"Not so, Jim. We do have compelling evidence and we will go to the grand jury. Those two men killed 265 people in Queens and we have the proof that they did just that. That is a fact that is not on your side. I expect you to tell me where they are so that we can make plans to pick them up on our homicide warrant."

There was silence for a minute.

"I'll get back to you, Judge. I have to climb up the ladder."

"The grand jury meets tomorrow morning. I expect to hear from you by noon with information about where we can pick up your two prisoners. They will remain in New York City or there will be some consequences for you and the justice department."

The conference call had not been a happy one for Jim Morrison. Some might say it had the potential to be a career-ender.

He was in his office at Federal Plaza in New York City, but all of the people on the other end of the line were in the nation's capital. He was glad that he did not have to face them in person with the news of Judge Bathgate's demand.

It was late at night, but he was more saddened than tired. He understood why the nation needed to know that the crash of flight 587 was due to pilot error and that there was no danger in continuing to fly American carriers. He understood that, but he could not see any end-game that would wind up proving that conclusion based on what Bathgate had told him and what his agents were learning about the evidence that pointed to the undebatable fact that the plane was brought down by a missile fired by the two men in federal custody. The cover-up that he was an integral part of was unraveling quickly and it was only a matter of time before the press frenzy began and both he and the NTSB were brought to heel for rushing to judgment and calling it a tragic accident caused by the first officer.

He had outlined Bathgate's demand and what his agents had learned about the evidence. There was a stunned silence when he was finished. He waited for somebody to speak.

"We have to put a lid on this," Tom Paine finally said after a long silence. "How do we do it? The Mayor, the Governor, who? I knew that Bathgate was not a team player, but this goes far beyond anything he should be doing."

"This is going to destroy the credibility of the Safety Board," Sherry Holmes said quietly. "How did they get that evidence? We thought we had everything locked up."

"Obviously, the NYPD detectives were better at getting the evidence than we were at covering it up," Morrison answered.

"Do you know what that evidence is," Paine asked. "Is it really as solid as Bathgate made it out to be?"

"At this point, I am not sure," Morrison said. "Fugate won't give me anything and the grand jury minutes will be sealed. It's going to be hard to pry that information loose. It seems that all the years of taking cases away from the city and refusing to give the NYPD information that it legitimately needed has caught up with us. verybody at One PP including the commissioner seem to believe that pay-back is fair game, especially with what they consider to be a mass homicide case. When this gets to the press, and notice that I said when and not if, this is going to be a bad hit. I think we have to backtrack and admit that we were quick to make the cause pilot error and say that new evidence developed by the New York cops has changed the picture."

"Can't do that Jim," Paine said. "The president and the nation has too much invested in the future of the aviation industry. That is not an option. We have to tough it out and say that the NYPD evidence, whatever it is, is manufactured."

Morrison sighed.

"Look Tom, I understand the need for the fiction and I even helped craft it, but my guys tell me there might even be a video of the missile bringing down 587."

"Videos can be easily faked today. We can discredit the evidence with our own evidence that there was no explosive residue on the wreckage. Can you keep your people in line, Sherry?"

"Of course we can, if they want to keep their jobs," Holmes said. "I have been assured that we hold all the debris in our possession. As far as I can discern, there is no other wreckage available that can prove that a missile brought down the aircraft. We are good to go."

"All right," Paine said. "Turn the men over to Bathgate for prosecution. He is going to come out of this looking like a clown, like that prosecutor in New Orleans on the JFK thing. Try and get a closer look at the NYPD's evidence so that we can refute it. If we go too Bigfoot on Bathgate now and it blows, we'll all be out of our jobs."

The connections were closed.

Morrison knew in his gut that they were wrong, but he had not reached his leadership position by refuting the White House. He would do what he could and get ready to leave the ship when it began to sink – as he was sure it would not long after the grand jury did its job and the two men were indicted, which would make everything public.

XIX

It had been an unproductive morning for Tom Paine.

A call to the mayor of New York was disappointing. The conservative mayor had told Paine that he would not, could not, interfere with the Queens DA, that he had been informed of the Grand Jury that would meet at 10 a.m. and that he concurred that the prosecution of the two men for numerous capital murders should go forward.

That the mayor was a former prosecutor himself did not help, nor did pleas that they were both of the same party do any good.

He held out hope that the mayor would tell his police commissioner to stop the investigation and quash the evidence. This obviously was not to be.

In the light of 9-11 and the war on terrorism, the crash of American Airlines Flight 587 had become larger than politics.

He did not relish going to the president to report that he had failed in stilling the investigation and prosecution of the two terrorists. Perhaps Jim Morrison was right. It was time to cut their losses and take some credit for stopping two terrorists who had already brought down one airliner. He would pitch that to the president when he saw him later in the day.

<hr>

Miquel Mercado was nervous, but had been working towards this morning for a long time.

The young assistant district attorney had been with District Attorney Andrew Bathgate for several years, working his way up from the intake bureau to the trials bureau. His job was to bring major cases before a grand jury made up of citizens and to convince those citizens to provide a True Bill, an indictment that would then be taken to trial by a more-experience assistant district attorney.

He had worked with the NYPD detectives and his supervisors to outline the evidence and decide what evidence would be sufficient to convince the grand jury that they should present the true bill for trial. He had to put the two terrorists at the point of the crime, show that they had the means and the motive to commit the crime, much like what he had to prove in any crime. This was special, he knew. The murder of that many people made it a national crime and, even though his name would never be noted in the newspaper, he was proud to be a part of it.

He reviewed what he had.

He had forensic evidence that put the terrorists in the rental car that went to the marina, on the boat that went out to Jamaica Bay that day, testimony from the woman who had facilitated their crime and most of all, the video of the missile coming from that boat that had exploded at the plane and the testimony of the person who shot the video, the toughest part of the evidence because the person who shot it was officially dead in the ruins of the World Trade Center.

He was sure that video alone and the reluctant testimony of the man who shot it would insure the true bill. He was eternally grateful that Bobby Sallow had agreed, at his own peril, to testify to the grand jury. He saw on his office clock that it was 9:45 a.m. and time to go to the jury room. He picked up all his files and checked once again that the video player was set up and ready to go. He fingered the DVD that would make his case and turned to leave for the jury room down the hall.

—— ((●)) ——

As Mercado walked out of his office door at the Queens Criminal Court, Detectives Billy Droesch and Richie Cohen sat outside the grand jury room, talking with both Ken and Ron Staller. Zeata, who had facilitated the terrorists in their Brooklyn safe house sat a little to their left, accompanied by Detective Tanya Pinto, who had been in on the takedown of the two terrorists. Still further away, sitting by himself was Bobby Sallow and across the hall from him, Ed Lopat, the rouge NTSB investigator who was ready to testify that debris from the plane did show explosive residue and that his agency was disingenuous about the reason for the crash.

Lopat hoped that he would not have to testify today. He knew that his testimony meant he would lose his job, although as a whistleblower, he had some cover. He knew that neither the two terrorists nor their attorneys would be there. It was a one-sided presentation with the jury hearing only what the prosecutor want-ed them to hear – just enough to rule that a crime had been com-mitted and that the two men had committed that crime.

Given that, they might well not need his testimony, but he was committed and wanted to be there just in case.

A man in jeans and a hoodie walked down the hall towards the jury room, passed it, took a drink of water from the fountain at the end of the hall and then walked slowly back down the hall slow-ly, seemingly on his cell phone, which Lopat thought was strange, since cell phones and other recording devices were not allowed anywhere near the wing were the grand jury hearings were held.

The thought struck the long-time federal investigator who had been a member of the Navy's NCIS before joining the NTSB that the man was federal, probably FBI, and that he was quietly taking photos of all the people sitting on the benches lining the hallway outside the grand jury room.

He was about to say something when Billy Droesch beat him to it.

The NYPD detective moved toward the man, bumping him as he passed by in the narrow hallway.

"Sorry," Droesch said showing his shield. "Can I ask you what you are doing with that cell phone? This is a restricted area."

The man turned towards Droesch and told him to fuck off, turning to walk away. Droesch snatched the phone from the man's hand and it hit the floor with a loud crack as the screen shattered on the tiles.

The man took a swing at Droesch but Cohen had joined the fray and pinned the man's arm.

Cohen handcuffed him.

Droesch picked up the phone, and saw that it was unlocked. He scrolled to the phone's photo album and found pictures of all the people sitting in the hallway.

"You're under arrest," Droesch said, already knowing that he had arrested a low-level federal officer. He wanted to send a message however, and he called for a court officer to take the man into custody. As he patted the man down, he found a Glock automatic pistol and a credential case showing the man was indeed and FBI agent.

He explained to the court officer, who took the man away. As far as Droesch was concerned, the law was the law. He wanted to make sure that the agent and his bosses would be sufficiently embarrassed to stop the surveillance. He wanted to send the agent back to his bosses with his tail between his legs. May he would even drop a hint about the incident to the New York Post.

<hr>

One by one, the men and women in the hall were called to testify before the grand jury. The testimony and the showing of the video clip, backed up by Sallow's testimony, took more than two hours.

Everybody waited in the hall for the decision. Finally, the blue light over the door came on. The grand jury had voted a true bill and had effectively arraigned the two men and sent them for trial.

Droesch was celebrating with the others on the steps of the Kew Gardens courthouse when his cell phone rang. He listened for a few minutes, said thank you and clicked off.

"The two perps were turned over to NYPD detectives twenty minutes ago," he said. Looks like the feds have given up. It's official that they are being held for the homicides involved with the Flight 587 crash. The DA will issue a press release as soon as it can be written and emailed to all the papers on his distribution list.

Rob Staller ran to his car. He had to get back to the Beachcomber and get a story out, at least on the web. The paper had come out that day and he would do a full, first-person story the following week.

His son, Ken, was in a rush as well.

He called Reaza Mohibir, who he had been dating for nearly a month.

She answered her cell on the first ring, already knowing that a call one way or another would be coming by early afternoon, enough time to get the story in the Saturday editions. In fact, as an insider, she had already written the story and was just waiting to add a lead that would tell that they terrorists had either been arraigned or not.

"Yes," she said expectantly.

"It's a go, 265 charges of felony murder," Ken said. "Call the DA's PIO office in ten minutes. They are writing a press release that might come out later, but you have all that information. Just get a quote and go with the story."

"Love you," she said.

"You too," he answered and clicked off. He knew she had a lot of work to do and then take the story to her editor, who would want some confirmation before publication.

Reaza turned to her computer and quickly brought up the story slugged "Terrorist AA 587" and added her lead.

She dialed her land line phone, calling the public information office for the Queens DA, a number she had called often in her job at Newsday.

"DA's office," a woman's voice answered.

"Reaza Mohibir from Newsday," she answered. "Can you run two names for me??

"Just a minute," the voice said, booting up her computer to the correct screen. "Go ahead."

She gave the names of the two terrorists, last name first, spelling them phonetically.

"How did you get this so fact," the voice asked with a chuckle. "Just got the charging documents five minutes ago."

She confirmed the arraignment and the charges against the two men.

"Could you fax me the charging documents," Reaza asked, giving her fax number.

"Sure, just give me a few minutes. You're the first one over the line. Must have a source inside, but that's OK. We want this to go wide."

"Can I get a quote from the DA," Reaza asked.

"We'll have a press release out in an hour or so," the voice said. "That will include quotes, but I don't have one to give you now. I'll make sure that you are one of the first to get the release."

Reaza said thanks and hung up. She printed out a copy of her story and made her way to the editor's office. She knocked and was told to come in.

"I have a big story for you, probably a front page that every paper in the nation will have tonight or tomorrow morning," she said. "I have it tight, corroborated just now by the DA."

Rob Moran, the Metro Editor, read the copy and then read it again.

"If this is real, it's the story of the year," he said.

He picked up his phone and dialed an extension. "Get up here right now," he said. "I have a story on your beat and I am wondering why you don't have it."

Jeff Toborg, the paper's aviation beat writer walked into the office, took one disdainful look at Reaza and then at Moran, who handed him the story. He read it quickly.

"Bullshit," he said, looking at Reaza. "I spoke with Sherry Holmes at NTSB and John McGraw at American just yesterday and they both warned me that some rumors were floating around but that they were not true. They have evidence of the pilot error and that is the cause of the accident."

"Then why were the two men who were arrested for trying to bring down that Air Bus plane just arraigned by the Queens DA on 265 charges of murder?" Moran asked.

Toborg had no answer.

Moran picked up the phone and called the DA's direct office number.

"Judge, its Rob Moran at Newsday," he said when he got Bathgate on the line. "I have a reporter with a story about flight 587 and two men arraigned. Correct?"

"Yes, we have solid evidence and are moving towards a trial"

"What do you say to the NTSB, who continues to say that the crash was an accident caused by the first officer?"

"I would say that the NTSB is either stupid or lying," the angry DA said, knowing that the quote would lead the story, but he no longer cared.

"Thanks, judge," Moran said and hung up the phone.

He scribbled some notes on Reaza's story and said, "Add this to your lead. You're our wood tomorrow, using an old journalist term for the front page."

He turned to Toborg.

"She beat you in your own territory," the editor said. "We'll talk about it tomorrow. Meanwhile, help Reaza all you can on getting some sidebars on the crash for tomorrow's paper."

The two left the editor's office without a word, Toborg glaring as Reaza as he walked away. He knew, however, that he had two choices – use his contacts to help with the sidebar stories that would accompany the main story written by Reaza or put in his resignation. He had been beaten on one of the biggest stories of the year and he didn't know how she did it. At the very least, he thought, his airline contacts, airline friends really, should have given him a heads-up.

＝＞＝«()»＝＜＝

The story broke on the cable and network stations that night, with CNN doing an hour-long story of the arraignments, tied to the Jet Blue takedowns and whatever information they could get from the DA.

CNN called all of the detectives involved with the Jet Blue takedown, but none of them would go on camera to speak about American Airlines Flight 587.

The next morning, Reaza's story broke on the front page of Newsday, detailing how she had found Zeata, the Muslim woman who had facilitated the terrorists while they were in Brooklyn and detailing the evidence against the two – the rental car, the boat, the video.

She appeared on Channel 2 and CNN and, because she was herself a Muslim, she was added to CNN's regular panel of experts that could be called on to testify about terrorist activity.

Her story went viral in the online edition and some on the staff said that she deserved the Pulitzer Prize for her work on the story.

An organization representing the passengers of TWA Flight 800, who were killed in July of 1996 in a tragic crash off Long Island, in which hundreds of eyewitnesses testified that the saw a missile rise into the sky and impact the airplane, demanded that the NTSB reopen the investigation which found that a faulty center fuel tank ignited, causing the tragedy. They used the fact that the NTSB was so wrong on AA 587 as evidence of the agency's failure to tell the truth.

"Stupity or cupidity" became their motto.

⸺•⟨●⟩•⸺

That afternoon, Ken Staller and Reaza met at the Belle Harbor Steak House in Rockaway.

They had a nice steak dinner. He had a beer, she had iced water.

They sat together and held hands.

"You know, the first time you told me you love me was when I told you to go ahead with the 587 story," he joked. "Do you love me for me or for the story?

She smiled and squeezed his hand.

"You know the answer to that question," she said, leaning over and giving Ken a long kiss.

They finished, paid the bill and went to Ken's apartment for desert. Reaza spent the night and the next day, the two got engaged.

⸺•⟨●⟩•⸺

The next day, Tom Lopat was fired from the NTSB after his name appeared in Reaza's story. It was expected. CNN had called him the day before and invited him to come on air and talk about the investigation and his part in bringing about the arrest of the two terrorists.

When they learned of his background, they offered him a job as commentator on aviation affairs. He took the job gladly and it paid three times what he was earning with the NTSB.

One of his first assignments was revisiting the crash of TWA 800, an investigation in which he had a part in 1996.

⸺•⟨●⟩•⸺

On December 2, the NTSB issued a press release saying that it was standing behind its findings in the AA 587 crash that the first officer over-used the rudder, tearing the tail off the plane.

Sherry Holmes went on cable TV to say that the Queens DA had no evidence and she looked forward to the trial so that she could refute whatever evidence he thought he had. She added that she stood by her agency's investigators, who were the best in the world at what they do.

The debris from the crash was transferred from Floyd Bennett Field in the dead of night and disappeared into the federal morass, never to be seen again.

The trial of the two terrorists on charges of attempted murder in the Jet Blue event and felony murder in the AA 587 case was set for early in mid-January of 2002.

It was an anticipated event.

All of the police officers and detectives involved in the investigation and arrests of the two terrorists were presented with the key to the city and with department medals.

That afternoon, they went back to work.